The K
in the Satir

Nancy strode into the living room, showing off new satin jacket.

Carson Drew cocked his head to one side. "Nan, you're a real knockout in that."

"I'm glad you like it," Nancy said, tucking her hands into the pockets shyly.

"Well, it's definitely retro," Carson said. "When was this look originally in style?"

Nancy's fingers brushed a scrap of paper in one pocket. Curious, she pulled it out. "Maybe this will answer your question," she said, unfolding it. "Here's a receipt, dated 1945."

Her dad took the yellowed receipt from Nancy and read it. "It's for a safe-deposit box at Mohegan Savings and Loan."

Nancy took the paper back from her father and began to tuck it into her pocket. Her hand struck something hard.

"There's something else here, too." Nancy grasped a lump in the pocket seam. Her fingertips pressed against it, exploring the flat, two-inch-long object— disc-shaped at one end, a shaft at the other.

"It's a key!"

Nancy Drew
Mystery Stories

Available from MINSTREL Books

NANCY DREW® 152

THE KEY IN THE SATIN POCKET

CAROLYN KEENE

A MINSTREL® BOOK

Published by POCKET BOOKS
New York   London   Toronto   Sydney   Singapore

This book is a work of fiction. Names, characters, places and incidents
are products of the author's imagination or are used fictitiously. Any
resemblance to actual events or locales or persons living or dead is
entirely coincidental.

A MINSTREL PAPERBACK *Original*

A Minstrel Book published by
POCKET BOOKS, a division of Simon & Schuster Inc.
1230 Avenue of the Americas New York, NY 10020

Copyright © 2000 by Simon & Schuster Inc.

ISBN: 0-671-03871-0

First Minstrel Books printing January 2000

10 9 8 7 6 5 4 3 2 1

NANCY DREW, NANCY DREW MYSTERY STORIES,
A MINSTREL BOOK and colophon are registered
trademarks of Simon & Schuster Inc.

Cover art by Ernie Norcia

Printed in the U.S.A.

Contents

THE KEY
IN THE SATIN POCKET

1

A Blast from the Past

"Keep your eyes open, guys," Bess Marvin said, peering out of the window of Nancy Drew's Mustang. "It's here on the left . . . at least, I think it is."

The three friends—Nancy, Bess, and Bess's cousin George Fayne—cruised slowly in the spring warmth along a leafy River Heights side street lined with small, older houses. "It's a cute little shingled house, painted robin's-egg blue," Bess recalled. "And there's a wooden sign hanging on a post out front—"

George piped up from the backseat. "Is that it, on the next block?"

Bess leaned forward, shading her eyes. "Yes!" she said happily. "The Telltale Heart!"

Nancy drove toward the sign Bess pointed to.

She heard George chuckle behind her. "The Tell-tale Heart? Like the Edgar Allan Poe story we read in high school? That was pretty gruesome, I remember. What does this store sell—poison, daggers, and manacles?"

"No, I already told you," Bess said. "It's a vintage-clothing boutique."

"You mean like a thrift store?" George said.

Bess rolled her eyes. "No, George. A thrift store just sells worn-out clothes that are out of style. These are vintage clothes—beautifully preserved treasures from another era."

"Seems to me the main difference is the price tag," George teased her cousin. "There's nothing thrifty about buying vintage clothes."

Bess sniffed. "Wait till you see this place, George. Then you'll change your attitude."

Nancy pulled the Mustang to the curb in front of a tidy blue bungalow. Racks of women's clothing were set out on the wide front porch, and straw hats dangled from the curlicued wooden porch trim. In one front window, bright Hawaiian shirts and bowling shirts were pinned at rakish angles. In another hung a bouffant powder-pink prom dress.

"I may not be a shopaholic like you, Bess," Nancy said as she climbed out of the car, "but I have to admit, this place does look like fun."

Bess bounded up the porch steps ahead of her friends. "You bet. And the great thing is, they're always getting in new stuff. Who knows what new treasures have arrived since I was here last week?"

Nancy and George stopped on the porch to admire a bunch of old-fashioned lace petticoats and camisoles on a rolling rack. Bess had already disappeared inside the cottage. Following her, Nancy and George entered a cozy warren of little rooms, each one cluttered with castoffs from a different era. George wandered into a sunny side room, originally the dining room, now full of 1960s clothes. Hidden speakers softly played folk rock to set the mood. "Wow, flowered hip-hugger bell-bottoms!" George said to Nancy. "And look at this Day-Glo yellow minidress. It would go great with those shiny white boots."

"Those were called go-go boots," a long-haired young woman spoke up from the hallway. She patted the mohair serape she was arranging on an old department-store mannequin. "They were the groovy thing to wear to go-go clubs—that's what some people called discos in the sixties."

Nancy drifted back to the front room, where the music was a restful piano sonata. Though Nancy reminded herself that she wasn't going to buy anything, she had to admit that the Telltale Heart was a cool place to hang out. She joined Bess, who was leaning intently over a display case full of filigree jewelry. "Some of these pieces date back to Victorian times. They're real antiques," Bess said.

3

"That big pin with the milky white stone is pretty," Nancy said, peeking over her friend's shoulder.

"That's a brooch, not a pin," Bess said. "And I think the gem is a moonstone. Right, Ada?"

The long-haired woman—apparently the store owner—strolled over to them. "Right, Bess. Moonstones were very popular with the Victorians. So were cameos, but I don't have any good cameos right now. Maybe I'll get some in soon. It's always worth checking back."

Nancy smiled, noting that Ada already knew Bess's name. She can tell a good customer when she sees one, she thought to herself.

Nancy wandered toward the back of the little house, brushing her hand over all the different fabrics as she passed: soft furs, muted velvets, slick satins, crisp taffetas, filmy gauzes. She followed the melancholy crooning of an old Frank Sinatra song into a small nook with dark wallpaper and wood-slat blinds. Sunlight fell on the faded carpet in narrow stripes, a lighting effect like something from an old black-and-white movie. The music came from a black vinyl LP spinning on a turntable in one corner. Clothes from the 1940s and 1950s hung from Art Deco wall sconces.

Nancy sang under her breath along with the old record as she browsed among the clothes. She was intrigued by a worn leather bomber jacket with authentic battle patches on its sleeves. From the high price tag, Nancy guessed it might be a genuine relic of World War II. She fingered the scarred leather, imagining the grim scenes the wearer of the jacket had witnessed. Beside it hung a navy and white polka-dot dress with padded shoulders and a long draped skirt—just what the pilot's girlfriend might have worn to welcome him home.

This is as good as a museum, Nancy thought as she worked her way down the rack. Each dress, blouse, shirt, and jacket seemed to have its own history. She stopped thinking of them as things to wear and saw them as windows into the past. The boxy cut of the clothes, the stout fabrics, the muted colors, all spoke of another time and place.

Then Nancy's eye fell on a flash of soft blue satin, wedged between nubbly tweeds and dark cottons. She slid the hangers apart to find a hip-length jacket, nipped in slightly at the waist. The fabric was a gorgeous lustrous satin, shot through with a pattern of lighter blues. It was a color Nancy had always loved, even before she realized that it brought out the blue in her eyes.

As she lifted the jacket off the rack and held it in front of herself, Nancy looked up and saw her reflection in a cheval glass. The jacket set off her red-gold hair perfectly. "Well, it won't hurt to try it on," Nancy murmured. "It probably won't fit, anyway."

Nancy set down her purse and shrugged off her fleece parka, then took the jacket off its hanger.

She slid one arm into the sleeve. The cool satin lining sailed over her skin. Putting her other arm in, she felt the jacket slip effortlessly onto her shoulders. It hugged her slim figure as though it had been tailor-made for her. Pivoting, Nancy saw in the mirror how flattering it was. Nancy felt like a vintage movie star in the jacket.

Nancy took it off quickly. She hadn't planned to buy anything today, not even something that looked fabulous on her. "I don't need any more clothes," Nancy muttered, shoving the hanger back into the jacket. She hung it on the rack with a clatter, scooped up her purse and parka, and hurried toward the front of the store.

She found George in the hallway, admiring herself in a lime green rib-knit sweater and a short orange vinyl skirt with lace tights. "Dig this," she said with a giggle. "All I need is a ton of mascara, white lipstick, and a long black wig, and I could be a lookalike for early Cher."

The shop owner turned around from a bureau in the corner. "Try this with it," she suggested to George, holding out a brightly patterned silk scarf. "The designs on it are totally psychedelic."

"George, you aren't thinking of buying that outfit, are you?" Nancy asked, eyebrows raised. "It's not exactly your style."

"Maybe not the whole outfit," George said defensively, draping the scarf around her neck, "but

6

at least the sweater. It's only ten dollars, and Ada says it's never even been worn."

Bess crossed the hall, a few items of clothing draped over her arm. "Ada, I'm taking these into the dressing room," she announced. "Find anything, Nancy?"

Nancy shrugged. "There's lots of neat stuff here, but I wasn't planning to spend any money today."

"You've got to try things on," George protested. "That's half the fun—to see yourself duded up. It's like going through a time warp."

Nancy recalled seeing herself in the mirror. "I did try on one thing—a blue satin jacket. If it's still here next time I come, maybe I'll buy it."

"How much?" Bess asked.

"I didn't even look at the price," Nancy said.

Bess rolled her eyes. "You have more sales resistance than anyone I know, Nan," she declared as she headed for the dressing cubicle.

"That blue jacket is stunning," Ada said to Nancy. "Several customers have tried it on, but it was too small for them. If it fits you, you'd better snap it up before someone else does."

"Yeah, Nan, this isn't a department store where they have six copies of everything in every size," George pointed out. "These are one-of-a-kind items. Once a garment is gone, it's gone."

Nancy crossed her arms. "But I promised myself I wouldn't buy anything. . . ."

"At least let me see it on you," George begged, grabbing Nancy by the elbow. "It's only fair, since you got to see me in this goofy getup."

Nancy led George back to the 1940s nook. The blue satin seemed to gleam out from the rack. Her fingers caressed the shimmering fabric as she took the jacket off the rack. Again she slipped it on over her shirt. Behind her, she heard George gasp slightly. "Nan, that is *you!*" George exclaimed.

Nancy gazed at herself in the mirror. "It really does suit me," she admitted. "It's a good color, isn't it?"

Bess popped her head around a nearby archway. "I was wondering where you two— Oh, Nancy!" she interrupted herself to exclaim. "Where did you find that? It is so excellent!"

"Maybe I should break down and buy it," Nancy said with a sigh of surrender.

"If you don't, I'll never speak to you again," Bess declared. "I think you were destined to own that jacket, Nancy. There's something about it. . . ."

At the Drew home that evening Nancy strode into the living room, pirouetting like a runway model. The Drews' housekeeper, Hannah Gruen, clapped her hands. "Nancy, I love it!"

Carson Drew, seated in his favorite armchair, cocked his head to one side. "Is that my daughter?"

he said in mock surprise. "Nan, you're a real knockout in that."

"I'm glad you like it," Nancy said, tucking her hands into the pockets shyly. "I felt extravagant buying it, but it was only fifty dollars."

"You'd never get a new jacket like it for that price," Hannah said, rising to examine the jacket. "Imagine how many years this has been sitting in someone's closet, not being worn just because it's 'out of style.' But a classic like this never really goes out of style."

Carson Drew seemed a little skeptical. "Well, it's definitely retro," he said. "When was this look originally in style?"

Nancy's fingers brushed a scrap of paper in one pocket. Curious, she pulled it out. "Maybe this will answer your question," she said, unfolding it. "Here's a receipt, dated 1945."

Her dad took the yellowed receipt from Nancy, and read it. "It's for a safe-deposit box. Number 49987 at Mohegan Savings and Loan." He looked up. "Mohegan closed down, didn't it, Hannah?"

Hannah pursed her lips. "Oh, yes—about twenty years ago, I think."

Delighted, Nancy took the paper back from her father. "How about that—a piece of history, right there in my pocket! That's a bonus you wouldn't get with a new jacket from the mall."

Nancy refolded the brittle slip of paper and

began to tuck it back into her pocket. Her hand struck something hard. She frowned.

"What is it, Nan?" her father asked.

"There's something else here, too." Nancy grasped a lump in the pocket seam. Her fingertips pressed against it, exploring the flat, two-inch-long object—disc-shaped at one end, a shaft at the other.

"It's a key!"

2

More Than Meets the Eye

"A key?" Carson Drew looked intrigued. "A key to what?"

"I can't get it out of the pocket," Nancy said, fumbling with the key. "It seems to be stuck inside the seam."

"Take off the jacket and turn that pocket inside out," Hannah Gruen said briskly, rising to fetch her sewing box. "Maybe a key got trapped inside a hole in the pocket. We can fish it out, then sew the pocket back up."

Nancy took off the jacket and turned the satin pocket inside out. "I don't see any hole," she said. "But there are extra stitches here, as if someone had mended the pocket already."

Hannah took the jacket from Nancy and peered

11

closely at the seam. "Big ragged stitches, too—as if they were made by someone who didn't know how to sew or had bad eyesight or was in a hurry. The thread is a different color from the jacket," she observed. She whisked out a tiny steel hook and began to prick the stitches apart. "Polyester thread—not good old-fashioned silk, like the original. This was definitely sewn more recently than 1945."

"I'll bet that key isn't there by accident," Nancy said. "It looks as if someone sewed it into the pocket deliberately, doesn't it, Hannah?"

Hannah dug her fingers into the opened seam and pushed out the tip of the flat shape. She grabbed it with her fingertips and extracted a small brass key, holding it up for Nancy and her father to see.

Carson Drew stood up to get a closer look. "It looks like the type of key used on safe-deposit boxes," he said.

"Then it must match the receipt!" Nancy said triumphantly.

"Let's not jump to conclusions," Mr. Drew cautioned. "If we hadn't also found that receipt, maybe the idea of a safe-deposit box wouldn't have crossed my mind. There could be several other uses for a key of this size."

Nancy took the key from Hannah. "But suppose someone left the receipt here along with the key as a clue to what the key was for? It's far-fetched, but . . ."

Her father smiled. "I know you love a mystery, Nancy," he said, "and you're as good a detective as anyone I know. But don't go imagining new cases where there are none. We have a key, and we have an old safe-deposit slip, for a bank that's gone out of business. The lock that this key once fit may not even exist anymore. And even if it does, it's probably not part of anything significant."

"Okay, okay," Nancy grudgingly agreed. "But I can't help wondering about it. A key without a lock is like a question without an answer. I just wish I knew, that's all."

"Ada will be surprised to see us back so soon," Bess remarked early the next afternoon as the three girls got out of Nancy's Mustang in front of the Telltale Heart.

"Remember, we're not here to buy anything," George warned her cousin. "You spent enough money yesterday."

The boutique owner, Ada Charriez, met the girls in the doorway of the blue bungalow. "Those cameos haven't come in yet," she told Bess. "Try again on Saturday."

"We didn't come about the cameos. It's about this coat," Nancy said, spreading her arms to display her satiny jacket. Her instincts told her not to mention the receipt and the key yet.

Ada frowned. "Was there anything wrong with it? It fits you like a dream. And it's in great condition, for a piece that old."

"No problem," Nancy reassured her. She tugged on the sleeves. "I just love it so much, I hoped you'd have some matching pieces."

Ada stared at the jacket, trying to remember. "A couple of weeks ago I got a ton of stuff from a secondhand dealer. Most of it was from the forties. I'm not sure, but I think I remember taking that jacket out of a cardboard box in that batch. Want to see some of the rest of that stuff?"

"Yes, please," Bess said eagerly, and Ada led them back to the 1940s nook. "There was a quilted-velvet dressing gown in a beautiful emerald green," she said, hunting through the racks, "but I think that's already been sold. There were several gabardine suits in the box, I recall. And look here." She pulled up a pair of cream-colored linen blouses, both embroidered with a monogram in pale lavender. She held them up against Nancy's jacket.

"Those are lovely," Nancy said, fingering the fine linen. "Do you suppose they were from the same owner?"

"No telling for sure," Ada said. "They're similar in style and size, though. If I had to make a guess, I'd say yes. They'd go great with that jacket. Add these and you'd have a perfect outfit." She lifted a hanger with a pair of fawn-colored trousers. "They're part cashmere."

As George stroked the trousers, her eyes lit up. "Wow, I've never felt wool this soft."

"Is that from the same box?" Nancy asked Ada.

Ada shook her head. "No, I picked those up at a garage sale last weekend. But they're from the same era."

"Do you get a lot of your merchandise at garage sales?" Bess wondered.

The boutique owner shrugged. "Garage sales, church rummage sales, individual customers—I get clothes from all sorts of sources."

"But you said my jacket came from a dealer?" Nancy steered the conversation back to her subject.

Ada nodded. "Jack Ryman. He buys second-hand stuff in large quantities—from going-out-of-business sales, warehouses dumping outdated stock, old houses being cleared after someone dies. He sorts through it and sells various items to all sorts of stores."

"And he's here in River Heights?"

"Yes," Ada said with a wary glance. "But I get all his good clothes, really. And I don't think he sells to individual customers."

Nancy realized that Ada was worried about losing customers. She reached out and picked up the nearest small item—a green suede belt with an elaborate silver buckle. "I like this. It looks like it's from the forties too," she said.

"Oh, yes, a very distinctive piece," Ada said, her voice sounding relieved. "See how the buckle is shaped like a dragon? Chinese accents like that were very popular in the forties and fifties."

"Did it come from the same box as Nancy's jacket?" George asked.

"Oh, yes, definitely," Ada said.

Nancy guessed Ada was just saying that to clinch the sale, but the belt was only ten dollars, and the more Nancy looked at it, the more she liked its Chinese design. "I'll take it," she said. Ada gave her a smile and headed for the cash register.

"I'll catch up in a minute," George called out. "I've just got to try on these pants." She shot Nancy a guilty glance. "They're cashmere, Nancy."

Nancy grinned. "I'm sure they're a bargain, George."

Bess followed Nancy to the front of the store, carrying the two linen blouses. "I'll take these, Ada," she said.

Ada smiled at Bess. "A good choice. Just remember, hand wash or dry-clean only. A washing machine would destroy this fabric."

Bess held up the blouses for Nancy to admire. She pointed to the embroidery. "Check the initials, Nancy—S.S.A. That tells us whom these belonged to."

"Actually, Bess, it's S.A.S.," Ada said. "When the middle initial of a monogram is the biggest, it stands for the person's last name."

"I wonder what S.A.S. stands for," Bess mused.

"Maybe Jack Ryman can tell us," Nancy said hopefully. "Could you please give me his address, Ada? I'm, uh, interested in finding some record albums from the same period. He might have some from wherever he got these clothes."

Ada gave Nancy a curious glance. "He might. He has a loft crammed with unsold stuff. But Jack knows what's valuable when he sees it, and he usually sells it right away. Most of what's left is junk." She scrawled an address on the bottom of Nancy's sales receipt. "Good luck."

As soon as George had finished buying the cashmere slacks, the three girls got back in the Mustang and drove to the address Ada had given Nancy. Checking the building numbers with the sales slip, Bess said, "I think it's that building on the right."

George leaned forward from the backseat. "Are you sure? It looks awfully run-down. Half the windows are broken, and there are no lights on."

"Except for the top floor," Bess noted. "And Ada says Ryman's office is on the top floor."

"Well, secondhand junk isn't a high-profit line of

work," Nancy said wryly as she parked the car. "Besides, Ryman's customers are store owners, not the general public. They don't need a fancy showroom. In fact, they probably feel as if they're getting a super deal if they buy their stock in a hole like this." As she got out of the car, she added, "Be sure to lock the doors, okay, guys?"

George led the trio, pushing open a rusty steel door and entering the building. In the cramped, badly lit vestibule they saw Ryman's name handwritten on a piece of cardboard tacked to the wall. A red arrow had been painted on the wall beside it, pointing upward.

The girls instinctively stayed close together as they climbed the narrow stairway. The silence of the old building gave Nancy the creeps. On the second-floor landing, George accidentally bumped her head against the only light source, a bare bulb hanging down on a cord. The bulb swung crazily, casting circling shadows on the stairway.

"Is it my imagination, or do these stairs slant sideways?" Bess whispered.

"I'll bet the outside wall of the building has settled over the years," Nancy replied softly. "That's not unusual in these old riverside structures. The pilings they're built on have rotted with age."

"Well, it makes me dizzy," George declared. Forging on up the final flight of stairs, she gripped the splintered handrail. With a groan, the brackets tore out of the crumbling plaster wall. George lurched backward, almost losing her balance.

Nancy jumped, startled, as a man's voice barked from the floor above them. "I'm telling you for the last time," he spluttered angrily. "It's out of my hands now!"

3

Suspicious Minds

Nancy exchanged wary glances with Bess and George. Did that angry voice upstairs belong to Jack Ryman? she wondered. What was he quarreling about and with whom?

The girls crept up the last few stairs. The steel door at the top stood ajar. George pushed it open gingerly.

A man with a gray ponytail, seated at a battered steel desk, was snarling into the phone. "Leave me alone, will ya?" He slammed the receiver down hard.

Then he jerked around, noticing the girls in the doorway. He tilted his head back to stare at them through small wire-rimmed glasses. "Who are you, and what do you want?" he asked suspiciously.

Nancy cleared her throat. "We're looking for Mr. Ryman's office."

"You've found it," he replied. "You got something to sell?"

Nancy inched forward, staring at the amazing amount of clutter that filled the long loft. Rows and rows of ceiling-high metal shelves were crammed with cast-off clothes, shoes, books, magazines, records, tapes, furniture, dishes, pots and pans, tools, appliances. Faint sunlight struggled to pass through the filthy windows along one wall, but the room was gloomy and dark.

Jack Ryman hopped up, sticking his thumbs in the pockets of his ripped, faded jeans. "I said, have you got something to sell?" he repeated.

"Ada at the Telltale Heart sent us," Nancy explained. "I bought something you sold her. I'd like to know where you got it originally." Glancing down the room, she had a sinking feeling. Jack Ryman handled so much junk, he couldn't possibly remember where he'd found one jacket.

Ryman's eyes tightened. "What's your name?"

"Nancy Drew."

"And what was the item?"

Nancy tugged on the collar of her jacket. "This."

Ryman's eyes lit up.

He remembers it! thought Nancy with a leap of hope. But then something in his face closed up, as if he was too cagey to admit it. "Why do you want to know where I got it?"

"Because I really like it—" Nancy began.

Ryman crossed his arms and interrupted her. "So I should let you cut me out by buying direct from my sources?"

"No, not at all," Nancy said. "I just hoped you might contact your source again."

"I can search my records," he offered. "But why? If you want matching clothes, do they have to be from the same source?"

Nancy could tell she wouldn't get information from Ryman unless she gave him some. "I found something in the pocket of the jacket. I'd like to return it to the owner," she said.

Jack Ryman straightened. "What did you find?"

"That's for the owner to know," Nancy said, stalling. "But it's something she might want back."

The dealer snickered. "The owner doesn't want anything anymore. She's dead."

Nancy paused. "Oh. I'm sorry to hear it."

Ryman flopped down in his chair, tipped it back, and put his feet—shod in scuffed cowboy boots—on the desk. "The family broke up the household after the old lady passed on," he explained. "I unloaded everything for them—furniture, clothes, china, jewelry, the whole deal. This was a few months ago."

"Did they live here in town?" Bess asked.

"You know the old Sassoon estate, up Windridge Road?" Ryman said.

George spoke up. "I remember a stone wall and iron gates on Windridge."

"That's the place," Ryman said. "That big old mansion provided a good chunk of business for me." He picked up a ballpoint pen and tapped his desk. "So, what did you find in the pocket? The heirs might want it for a keepsake. I could return it to them for you."

Nancy shook her head. "If the heirs were interested in keepsakes, they wouldn't have sold the entire contents of the house."

Ryman chuckled. "That's true. They couldn't be the sentimental type. The old woman was hardly cold before they cleared out the joint."

"What are their names?" Bess asked.

"I don't know," Ryman admitted. "I didn't deal with the heirs directly. The mansion was sold to a man named Carl Haddon. He emptied the house to turn it into a boarding school. Haddon Hall, it's called."

"Could Carl Haddon put me in touch with the heirs?" Nancy asked.

"Probably." Ryman peered over his wire-rims at Nancy. "But tell me—I'm dying of curiosity—what *did* you find in that pocket? Normally I check all the clothes, but this was such a big load that I kind of rushed through it."

"Nothing special," Nancy said with a casual wave of her hand. "Just a little key."

Ryman halted, his eyes brightening. But he played casual, too, pulling some papers toward him and scribbling in the margins. "A key? It's probably useless. I'll bet all the locks up there got changed in the renovation." He held out a hand. "If you give it to me, I'll check it out. No need for you to bother."

"It's no bother," Nancy said crisply. Her hand tightened around the key in her jacket pocket.

Ryman's gaze narrowed. He still held out his hand. "Really, you can trust me. I've dealt with Haddon before—he knows me. It was nice of you to bring the key down, but I can handle the situation from here."

"That isn't necessary," Nancy replied, backing away. "I'll be happy to visit Haddon Hall. I'm curious to see the new school, anyway. Thanks for your help, Mr. Ryman."

Nancy turned and hurried out the door, with George and Bess close behind. They scurried down the stairs as fast as they could. Tumbling out onto the street, the girls breathed with relief. "That was starting to turn weird," George declared.

"He sure seemed eager to get the key from me," Nancy said, unlocking her car.

"Maybe he knows what it unlocks," Bess suggested as they climbed into the car.

"He's probably kicking himself for not noticing it when he had the jacket," George pointed out.

Nancy looked back at the warehouse. She saw a face peering down at them from the dirty top-floor window. It had to be Jack Ryman.

"Remember the conversation we heard before we walked in?" she asked her friends as she started the car.

Bess nodded. "It sounded like somebody was trying to get something from Ryman—something he didn't have anymore."

"Right," Nancy said. "Now, I know he deals in a lot of stuff. But he sure recognized this jacket. And he was awfully persistent about learning what I'd found in the pocket."

"Do you think the person on the phone was looking for your jacket?" George wondered out loud.

Nancy pondered the question as she pulled the Mustang away from the curb. "It's possible, isn't it? All I know is that the more I learn about this jacket, the more strange facts I turn up. My dad may be wrong—there could be a mystery in this after all."

"Jack Ryman said he sold lots of different stuff from the Sassoon mansion," Bess recalled. "Suppose I poke around some antique shops to see what else he unloaded?"

"And I can check out that safe-deposit receipt,"

George offered. "I know that Mohegan Savings Bank is closed, but somewhere there must be a record of what happened to its accounts."

"That'd be great," Nancy said. "Meanwhile, I'll go out to Haddon Hall. Carl Haddon should be able to tell me how to reach the Sassoon heirs. This is their key, after all, and they probably want it back."

After dropping off her friends, Nancy drove north of town and turned on to Windridge Road. She hadn't been out that way for a couple of years. Here and there, new housing developments had replaced the woods and farmland she remembered. Nancy felt a twinge of sorrow. "Why can't they just leave the countryside green and natural?" she muttered to herself.

Soon she hit a wooded stretch of road that seemed more familiar. Immediately after one sharp curve, the blue Mustang swung with a bounce over a small humpbacked stone bridge. "Ticklebelly Bridge!" She giggled, recalling the name her father had given it long ago during a Sunday drive.

Around the next curve Nancy spotted an iron gate between a pair of stone pillars—the gate George had mentioned earlier. There was a new sign, freshly painted, on the right-hand pillar: Haddon Hall.

Years ago the gates had been closed. They stood open now. With a surge of curiosity, Nancy drove through and headed up a long, tree-lined gravel drive. At the far end she spied a dark redbrick mansion with Tudor-style half-timbering, set on a rise of land in front of thick woods. Its diamond-paned windows glinted in the sunshine.

Nancy parked on an apron of gravel in front of the mansion and climbed out. Admiring the house, she headed for the massive pair of oak front doors. They stood ajar, letting sunshine stream into a grand entry hall with a diamond-patterned tile floor.

As Nancy stepped inside, a bell rang down a passageway to the left. She heard doors bang open; a swell of chatter arose. High school–age boys and girls strolled into the entry, talking eagerly and carrying textbooks. Halfway up an imposing carved-wood staircase, a girl leaned over the banister and called to two friends. Nancy smiled, enjoying the feeling of being back in school.

She tapped a passing boy on the shoulder. "Excuse me?"

He turned and looked at Nancy with dark, roguish eyes. "Hi. Are you new here?" he asked in pleased surprise.

Nancy shook her head. "No, I'm just a visitor. I'm trying to find Mr. Haddon."

The boy chuckled. "Haddon? You must be joking. He's never around. He's always off raising money or recruiting new students. Now that we've moved to this big new property, he's got to pay for it, I guess."

"Where was the school before?" she asked.

"Marston Falls," he said. "But it was too small, and then we had a fire last fall. Luckily Haddon found this place and fixed it up fast. We moved in a few weeks ago." He winked at Nancy. "Maybe you can show me around River Heights sometime."

"Maybe," Nancy said with a grin. "When Mr. Haddon isn't here, who's in charge?"

The boy sneered. "The headmistress, Ms. Chilton. Her office is down that hall." He jerked a thumb toward a pointed archway.

Nancy thanked him and headed down the hallway. The noise of the students grew fainter as she passed a handful of small offices. At the end of the hall, she found a name printed in gold letters on a door: Head of School, Vanessa Chilton. Nancy knocked. A voice within called, "Come in."

Nancy poked her head around the door. Behind a desk she saw a thin young woman with dark hair, dressed in a severely tailored dark suit. The woman looked up and put on a glazed smile. "Hello, I'm Vanessa Chilton." She rose and offered her hand to Nancy. "Won't you be seated?"

Nancy shook the headmistress's hand, then perched in a hard-backed chair across from her desk. "Nice to meet you. I'm Nancy Drew."

"Welcome to Haddon Hall. Have you had a chance to look around?" Ms. Chilton asked.

"Not yet," Nancy said. "But it looks like a beautiful place. I heard you moved in recently."

Ms. Chilton nodded. "Yes, but we've settled in quickly and the students are hard at work." She shifted in her chair. "Are, uh, your parents going to join us, Miss Drew?"

Nancy looked puzzled. "My parents? My dad's at work, and . . . my mother died when I was little."

A pained look flickered across Ms. Chilton's face. "I'm sorry," she said quietly. "But couldn't your father join us for the interview?"

"Interview?"

"Yes, you are applying for a place in our school, aren't you?" Ms. Chilton frowned.

Nancy chuckled, realizing the misunderstanding. "Oh, no. I've already graduated from high school— from River Heights High. I've just come to ask you about this house."

Ms. Chilton cupped her chin tightly with one hand. "Are you a reporter? I can't give interviews without Mr. Haddon's prior approval."

"I'm not a reporter," Nancy said. "I just want to know about the Sassoons, the people who used to live here."

"I know nothing about them," the woman declared briskly. "And I have no time to talk to you."

Just then a man's voice came through the doorway behind Nancy. "Ms. Chilton, I found a broken window at the back of the house," he said. Nancy twisted around to see a stocky fiftyish man in overalls. "There are muddy footprints below the window. I'll bet that's where he broke in."

Ms. Chilton jumped to her feet, clutching the desk with tense fingers. "Not *now*, Vernon," she snapped. Then she turned to Nancy, her face drained of all color. "I told you I had no time to talk. I must ask you to leave my office—immediately!"

4

The Break-in

Nancy stared into Vanessa Chilton's steely blue eyes. The headmistress seemed determined to kick her out. Why was she afraid of Nancy's questions?

Nancy rose to her feet. "Thanks for your time," she said grudgingly as she left the office. She would never get information from Ms. Chilton now.

When Nancy had walked a few steps down the hall, she heard Vernon shut the office door. Then she halted. The corridor was quiet and empty. No one would notice if she hung around.

She doubled back to the headmistress's office and pressed her ear against the door. She heard Vernon's gravelly voice say, "But, Ms. Chilton, ma'am, someone's bound to find out about the intruder—"

Ms. Chilton cut him off in an icy tone. "You don't understand the impact of that. We can't afford to lose any more students—we lost enough after the fire. If parents get the idea that we have poor security, they'll withdraw their children. We could be ruined."

"Security will be fine once the hardware is installed," Vernon insisted. "But Mr. Haddon was in such a hurry to move in that there wasn't time to finish all the renovations, let alone get the alarms wired. Once the police check out the break-in site—"

"Police?" Ms. Chilton's voice rose. "We don't want the police in on this."

Nancy heard a groan escape Vernon. "But, ma'am, a crime has been committed."

"How could the police help?" the headmistress asked. "The intruder's long gone. And nothing seems to be missing, so there's no stolen property to recover."

Nancy frowned, surprised. A break-in where nothing was stolen?

Just then she heard Vernon moving toward the door. She sprang away to avoid being caught eavesdropping. She sprinted up the hallway, reaching the entry hall before Vernon opened the office door.

Classes had started again; the school was quiet. Nancy looked around at the paneled walls and sweeping staircase. Now that I'm here, she told herself, it would be a shame not to have a look around. Jack Ryman said that the house had been renovated, but many original features appeared to be intact. Maybe the lock she wanted was still here. Nancy ran lightly up the grand staircase.

From the upstairs landing, two corridors stretched in either direction. Moving along one and then the other, Nancy found a series of large, square dormitories, each with five beds, five dressers, and five desks. One wing held boys' dorms, the other girls'. At the end of either hallway was a large communal bathroom, with a row of sinks and a row of showers.

From the freshly plastered walls, Nancy guessed that these rooms had been knocked together from the original bedrooms. The dormitory furniture was simple and bare, though students had added their own touches, with posters and bright bed-spreads. Nancy turned a doorknob and peeked into one room—no locks at all, let alone an old-fashioned one.

Nancy wandered back downstairs, where a bit more of the original flavor of the house had survived. A wide corridor with six rooms ran to the left of the entry hall. The handsome mahogany doors were shut now, but Nancy guessed these must have been drawing rooms and parlors at one time.

At the end of the hallway, a door stood open to a

vast library with bookshelves lining every wall. Tall windows at the far end overlooked a manicured lawn. Wandering in, Nancy studied the books on the shelves. She recognized many of them from the River Heights High library. These must have been brought from the school's previous site. The Sassoons had probably owned thousands of books, she mused, but Jack Ryman had sold them off to used-book stores.

Pivoting, Nancy noticed a fireplace on a side wall. Over it hung a life-size oil painting in an ornate gilded frame. She stood before it, studying the regal-looking young woman. Silky light brown hair, styled in a long pageboy, framed her lovely pale face. She wore a shimmering peach-colored evening gown and a lustrous strand of pearls. The proud tilt of her chin, the commanding look in her blue eyes, caught Nancy's attention. Who does she remind me of? she wondered.

Lost in thought, Nancy didn't hear the footsteps on the hallway carpet. High heels clicked suddenly on the library's parquet floor. Nancy jumped and turned to see Vanessa Chilton in the doorway. The headmistress stiffened with anger. "I thought I told you to leave," she said coldly. "Why are you still nosing around?"

"I was on my way out," Nancy replied, trying to sound innocent, "but I had to check out this gorgeous library. You certainly have a lot of books."

"Of course we do—we're a school," the headmistress said in clipped tones. "Now may I escort you from the property?"

Nancy walked along the corridor with Ms. Chilton behind her, feeling the woman's eyes boring into her back. Ms. Chilton waited on the doorstep, arms tightly folded, as Nancy got into her Mustang. Rolling down the driveway, Nancy glanced in her rearview mirror and saw the headmistress still standing there, staring intently at her departing car. She did not move until Nancy drove through the front gate.

"Whoa," Nancy muttered, "that woman doesn't trust anybody, does she? I'll bet she's incredibly unpopular."

She pulled her car to the side of the road to plot out a course of action. Vanessa Chilton's strange behavior made Nancy more eager than ever to investigate Haddon Hall. But how could she get in? The headmistress would run her off for sure.

Just then a silver delivery van swung around the nearby curve. Seeing Nancy's car, the driver honked and waved. Nancy looked up and realized she knew him—Ed Vascillero, who had gone to high school with her. She gave her horn a friendly beep and waved back.

Ed pulled his truck over and stopped. He leaned out his window to grin at Nancy.

"How are you doing, Ed?" Nancy called out.

"Doin' great, Nancy," Ed said with the wide, goofy grin she remembered.

"You're working for Pearson's now?" Nancy asked, gesturing toward the words lettered on the truck: Pearson's Laundry.

"Yeah, been working there since graduation," Ed said. "I'm going to college at night, at Riverview. What about you? Still in the detective business?"

Nancy smiled politely, though she preferred to keep her work quiet. "I do a little here and there. So where are you headed?"

Ed jerked a thumb toward Haddon Hall's gates. "I'm dropping off some laundry here. Every Thursday afternoon at five, I pick up a hamper of dirty laundry, just inside the back door. And I leave them a new hamper with clean sheets and towels, so they can change the beds tomorrow."

Nancy perked up. "You drop off the linens in a big hamper? How big?"

"Oh, I don't know—three feet by five feet, I guess." Ed glanced back into his van at the hampers. "They need a lot of sheets and towels."

Nancy paused, considering the idea that had just sprung into her head. Ed had always been a good guy, and she knew she could trust him. "Ed, can I ask you for a favor?" she asked sweetly.

Nancy rearranged her cramped limbs, trying not to crumple the crisp starched sheets beneath her.

When Ed had first shown her the inside of the wicker hamper, it had seemed roomy. Four hours later the space felt incredibly tight.

"Good night, Sally. You drive home safely," Nancy heard one of the kitchen staff call out to a fellow worker. Nancy had been listening to their voices for so long that she felt she knew them.

"Night, Edie." The cook's footsteps came close to the hamper. Nancy heard a series of clicks, and through the slits in the wicker she saw the kitchen lights snap off. She heard the cook's footsteps heading out the back entrance, then the clatter of the woman's keys locking the door.

Silence settled on the kitchen. Nancy checked her glow-in-the-dark watch: almost nine P.M. With the staff gone, she could test the lid of the hamper, which Ed had promised to leave unlatched. She raised it a couple of inches. So far so good. But I'd better wait another hour before prowling around, Nancy decided. It wouldn't do to get caught.

With a sigh she shifted her body again. Bess and George should be parked outside the front gates of the school by now—that is, provided Bess had gotten the message on her answering machine. Fortunately, Ed had had a cell phone, so Nancy had been able to call her friends before getting into the hamper. That seemed like a long time ago.

A moment later Nancy heard a harsh buzzer sounding upstairs. The lights-out signal, she guessed. But wasn't it awfully early? She checked her watch again—nine-thirty. She must have dozed off. She shook herself awake, listening to the silence in the building grow deeper and deeper.

She poised herself to crawl out of the hamper. Raising the lid, she extended one leg—

Wait! Those sounds on the far side of the kitchen door . . . were they footsteps? Nancy crouched low, remembering Vernon's words about a mysterious intruder.

Furtive footsteps and giggles came through the swinging door. "Are you sure it's safe, Kyra?" a girl whispered.

"As safe as it'll ever be" came a hushed reply.

Nancy put an eye to a small gap in the wicker. She saw three girls sneak into the darkened kitchen. "If Chilton catches us, we're cooked," one girl said, giggling.

"It's her fault," the tallest girl replied. "If they didn't serve such lousy food here, we wouldn't have to break in to get snacks."

With a groan, Nancy settled back against the sheets. She was relieved it wasn't the intruder, but she couldn't move until the girls left.

"The food was better when Mr. Warriner was headmaster," the girl named Kyra said, sighing. "I wish he hadn't retired."

"I didn't appreciate how nice he was until Chilton took over," the third girl said.

They passed close by the hamper on their way to the pantry. "See if you can find the oatmeal cookies," Kyra suggested.

"No, they're rock-hard and tasteless," the tall girl said. "Look for peanut butter."

"Hey, the pantry is locked!" the third girl declared. Nancy heard the rattle of a padlock.

"I told you, Chilton is so suspicious!" the tall girl scoffed.

"Now what do we do?"

"Starve, I guess," the tall girl said crossly. "Come on, guys, let's go back to bed before we get caught." Their footsteps scuttled back across the kitchen and through the swinging door.

Nancy remained where she was until she was certain they were gone. Finally she judged it was safe. She lifted the lid and stuck out a leg, gratefully feeling the blood rush into her tingling limbs.

Nancy tiptoed around the kitchen, cautiously training her penlight everywhere. There appeared to be nothing left from the Sassoon days; now there were only gleaming new appliances and cupboards. Working her way around the room, she found a door that looked like part of the original house. She pushed it open.

Inside was a large storage closet. Nancy switched on the light and glanced over the brooms, mops, and buckets near the door. Behind them were paint cans, odd pieces of plywood, and a paint-spattered drop cloth—left over from the renovation, Nancy guessed. She moved closer to check behind them.

A stack of posters slid to the floor, and Nancy bent down to pick them up. Paint drips on one side told her that the painters had used these as drop cloths. When she flipped one over, she saw colored-pencil drawings. She tilted the board for a better look at the heading: Shady Acres, Your Home for the Future.

Nancy grimaced as she studied the sketches. Rows of look-alike one-story houses in another boring housing development. This one will never be built, she mused, recognizing Haddon Hall's front gate. Carl Haddon's purchase must have saved this lovely old house from being razed to make way for Shady Acres.

Suddenly Nancy heard a tinkle of breaking glass. She froze. Was it another gang of hungry students? Or had the intruder returned?

She flipped off the light and went to the closet door to peer through the crack between the door and the frame.

A shaft of silver moonlight poured through one of the kitchen windows. Nancy saw a shadowy form huddled on the sill. It raised its arm to strike the windowpane again.

5

Who's Chasing Whom?

Nancy leaped forward. Every instinct told her to apprehend the burglar at the kitchen window.

The figure in the window, arm still raised, teetered wildly on the sill when Nancy jumped in front of him. She had a brief glimpse of a black ski mask and hooded sweatshirt; a hammer glinted in his gloved hand. Then the burglar fell backward, dropping out of sight.

I've got to catch him, Nancy vowed. She spun around and ran to the back door. After grabbing the knob, she flipped the thumb piece on the top lock, freed the dead bolt, and flung open the door.

Wee-ooh-wee-ooh-wannh! An electronic alarm shrieked into the night. "Good work, Vernon!" Nancy murmured. "You got the alarms wired just in time." She raced out into the crisp night air, following the dark figure into the woods.

The alarm continued to blare behind her as Nancy plunged into the woods. I should get some backup, thanks to that alarm, Nancy said to herself. Maybe even the police. And if I help catch the burglar, Ms. Chilton may change her mind about me.

The thick woods closed in around Nancy. Far ahead of her, she heard footsteps and a thrashing in the early-spring foliage. She followed the noises, listening intently as she made her way forward.

In the dark, though, it was hard to find her footing. Several times Nancy stumbled over roots or ran into low-hanging branches. The sounds ahead of her were getting farther and farther away. He knows his way through these woods, Nancy realized. He's been here before.

A few seconds later Nancy halted, straining her ears to determine where the intruder was. She could faintly hear voices shouting back by the school building, but she heard nothing more of the fleeing burglar. "I've lost him!" Nancy said, frustrated. Her body sagged with disappointment as she leaned against a tree.

She could still hear people shouting back by the main house, including a gruff voice Nancy recognized as Vernon's. A flashlight beam played over the trees at the edge of the woods. Nancy began to walk back to the school. At least I can tell them what I saw of the intruder, she said to herself.

Then Nancy heard Vanessa Chilton's shrill, anxious voice saying, "You're sure it was the girl who was here this afternoon?"

"Yes, ma'am," Vernon replied. "I'd recognize that blue jacket and that red-gold hair anywhere."

Nancy froze, pulling back into the shadows. They thought *she* was the intruder! That would be a logical conclusion, Nancy realized. She was the one who had set off the back-door alarm. Vernon must have spotted her as she ran into the woods. In the moonlight she'd have been clearly visible while the real burglar was hidden by the trees.

Even if she did convince them that she wasn't the intruder, Nancy thought, she'd have to explain how she got on the property. Being smuggled indoors in a linen hamper would look awfully suspicious.

"There's no way Vanessa Chilton will believe I'm innocent," Nancy muttered. "And now she'll really be on guard against me. There go my chances of searching the mansion." She turned and began to pick her way through the woods, away from the house.

Keeping the driveway on her left, Nancy stayed just inside the cover of the trees until she reached the edge of the property. She found a slender sapling growing beside the wall and used it to help her scale the wall. Nancy paused atop the wall for a moment, searching up and down the road for George's car. She spotted it fifty yards away, near the front gates, right where she had told her friends to meet her. She dropped to the ground and jogged toward them.

Huddled inside the dark car, George and Bess were startled when Nancy tapped on the window. Bess threw the back door open. "Nan! Are you okay? We heard the alarm go off and people shouting. Then a car parked down the road started up with a roar and screeched past us, as if the driver was trying to make a fast getaway."

Nancy jumped into the backseat and yanked the door shut. "A getaway? I'll bet anything that was the burglar I saw. I set off the alarm trying to chase him. Did you get a look at his car?"

"Well, it *is* kind of dark," George said, "and he rocketed right out of here. But I think it was a mid-size gray sedan, a recent model. I couldn't read the license plates, but the design was odd. Maybe they were out-of-state plates."

Nancy slammed a fist into her other hand. "That had to be the intruder! He tried to break in through the kitchen window while I was investigating. So now the folks at the school think *I'm* the burglar."

"A burglar?" George quirked an eyebrow. "This is a bizarre coincidence. You decide to steal into the school on the same day somebody else tries to break in. What's going on in that place?"

"That's what I'd like to know," Nancy said. "I gather this burglar was there once before, but for some reason the headmistress wouldn't call the police."

"Sounds fishy to me," Bess declared.

Nancy leaned back in the seat. "It sure does. I've got to find out what's going on. But for now I guess we'd better head home." She gazed wistfully at Haddon Hall's gates as George drove past them on the way back to town.

"Nancy, maybe this will cheer you up," George said. "I had some success this afternoon. I went through old newspapers in the public library and learned that when Mohegan Savings failed, it was absorbed by Midstate Federal Bank. All account holders had the option of transferring their accounts to Midstate. I thought I'd visit Midstate's main downtown branch tomorrow to see if there's a record of the safe-deposit number on that old receipt."

Nancy perked up. "It's a long shot, but it might lead to something. And for now, it's all we've got to go on."

Bess turned to give Nancy a curious look. "If you don't mind my asking, Nancy, what exactly are we looking for?"

Nancy set her jaw stubbornly. "That intruder is looking for something—maybe something the Sassoon family left in the mansion. He keeps coming back, so it must be something important. Anything that once belonged to the Sassoons could be significant."

"Like your jacket," George said.

"And the things you found in its pockets," Bess added. "And who knows what else?"

The next morning Nancy set off for the River Heights Bureau of Records. At the front desk she filled out a slip requesting probate records from the past five years under the name Sassoon.

The clerk punched several keys on his terminal, then frowned. "Nothing has been listed under that name in the past five years," he declared.

Nancy was puzzled. "But the Sassoon house was sold less than a year ago by the estate."

The clerk shrugged. "Maybe it was listed under another name. Maybe the last Sassoon was married and used a different last name. Let's do a global search for all Sassoon deaths in River Heights."

Nancy nodded, grateful that she had hooked up with a clerk who took pleasure in hunting for information.

The most recent Sassoon will they found was that of Sarah Sassoon. It had been brought to probate court six years earlier. The clerk called up a copy of the will on his terminal. "It says she had no living relatives," the clerk read. "She left everything to her paid companion, Delia Cox."

Nancy cupped her chin thoughtfully in one

hand. "Then Delia Cox must have been the owner who sold the Sassoon mansion to Carl Haddon. Is she still alive?"

The clerk punched keys. "Nope. She died a few months ago, last November eighteenth. Want me to call up her will?"

Nancy nodded, watching the screen intently as the clerk retrieved the will. "Here it is. According to this, she left all her possessions to her nephew, Roger Cox," Nancy said. "So it must have been Roger Cox who sold the property to Haddon."

"I can check the date of sale," the clerk said, his eyes sparkling with interest. "First let me switch to the program for real estate transactions."

"Thanks." Nancy hunkered down beside him at the terminal. Ten minutes later the clerk had finally found the real estate title transfer records. He entered the name Cox and waited. "Hmm."

"Hmm what?" Nancy asked.

"It wasn't Roger Cox," he reported. "It was Delia Cox who sold the house, plus one hundred acres of land, to Carl Haddon in a deal signed November thirteenth."

"November thirteenth?" Nancy exclaimed. "That was only five days before she died."

The clerk's eye flickered over the screen. "And get this. The purchase price was four hundred and fifty thousand dollars."

Nancy frowned. "But I've seen that house—it's worth at least a million dollars. It's a mansion!"

"Plus one hundred acres of prime land," the clerk said. "Carl Haddon got a deal, all right. Maybe Delia Cox was senile. The probate records showed she was eighty-two when she died."

Nancy tapped her cheek with one finger. "Could be. But many people in their eighties are perfectly rational. I wonder why she sold that property so cheap."

The clerk smiled apologetically. "I've got a lot of information in this computer, but not that kind."

"Thanks anyway," Nancy said, gathering her things. "You've been a lot of help."

Nancy walked from the bureau to Midstate Federal Bank, where she'd agreed to meet George at eleven-thirty. George was waiting on the sidewalk outside the bank, an imposing classical-style granite building. They strolled to a nearby coffee shop. Once they had settled in a booth and ordered lunch, Nancy told George what the public records had contained. "And Sarah Sassoon left the property to her companion, a woman named—"

"Delia Cox!" George broke in.

Nancy looked surprised. "You know her?"

"Listen to what I learned," George said. "When Mohegan transferred its accounts to Midstate Federal in 1967, our account—safe-deposit box number 49987—was transferred to Midstate, where the number on the account and the keys to the box remained the same. The name on the account at that time was S. Sassoon."

"Sarah Sassoon!" Nancy said.

"Right. But the box was later transferred to D. Cox." George looked triumphant. "I got a clerk—her name's Margo Rosnick, she's really nice—to show me the log in the safe-deposit vault, where account holders sign in. The clerk compares your signature to the one on file before she lets you open your box. Delia Cox signed in to visit box 49987 last November fifteenth."

"That was two days after she sold the mansion to Carl Haddon," Nancy noted. "And three days later she died."

George looked startled. "She's dead? But the bank thinks she's still alive. The records show that the annual fee on that box is paid up."

Nancy pushed away her half-eaten tuna melt. "Delia's executors must not have known she had that safe-deposit box. Otherwise, they'd have contacted the bank when the estate was settled." She chewed her lip. "What's the procedure to visit a safe-deposit box?"

"Margo explained it to me," George said, stirring her iced tea. "After you sign in, you need two keys—the account holder's and the bank clerk's master key—to open the locked box."

Nancy leaned across the table. "Did you see

what type of key she used? Did it look like the one I found?"

"Margo didn't show me a key, and I couldn't think of a way to ask her," George admitted. "She already divulged more information than she probably should have. Maybe I could go back on Monday and show her your key. Do you have it with you?"

"No, I left it at home, in my jewelry box, for safekeeping," Nancy said.

After leaving the coffee shop, the girls drove back to Nancy's house. Nancy unlocked the front door and headed first for the answering machine: "Hello, Nancy, this is Chief McGinnis." Nancy smiled at the police chief's familiar voice. His help had been crucial to her on many cases. "I checked into that matter you called me about earlier this morning. No, Haddon Hall has not reported any break-ins—not last week and not last night. Let me know what's up."

Nancy gave George a knowing glance. "See? The headmistress didn't report the break-in at her school. She has to be hiding something."

Then the second message came on. "Is this Nancy Drew's house?" came a muffled woman's voice. Nancy frowned, not recognizing it.

"I saw you downtown in your new jacket," the woman gushed. "It's so gorgeous, and I'd really love to buy it from you. Can we meet?"

6

Meeting with a Stranger

"Meet me tomorrow," the mysterious phone message went on. "One-thirty, in front of La Parisienne café, downtown at Main Street and Water Street. I'll wear a yellow hat. You wear the blue jacket." The message ended with an abrupt click.

George and Nancy shared a baffled look. Nancy punched the Replay button to listen to the message a second time. She held her breath, trying to detect any clues to the speaker's identity.

"I'll bet she was holding something over the mouthpiece to disguise her voice," she said. "She sounded rushed and nervous. The machine indicates that this call came through only ten minutes ago. I wish I'd been here to answer the phone in person."

"I wonder how she got your name and number," George mused.

Nancy shrugged. "Maybe she saw me at the Bureau of Records and asked the clerk who I was."

"It *is* a pretty jacket—it's not surprising someone would want to buy it," George reminded Nancy, gently touching the silky sleeve.

Nancy shook her head. "But you don't see someone wearing a jacket and just assume it's for sale. Besides, any normal buyer would leave a name and number where I could reach her."

"You wouldn't sell that jacket, would you?" George said.

"Never—especially not now, with all this mystery surrounding it." Nancy grinned. "But I am tempted to meet the caller anyway, just to see who she is and why she wants my jacket. You never know—this could break the case wide open."

"So, Nancy, you're interested in my former client Delia Cox," said her father's friend Evan Tyrell, a prominent River Heights attorney. He was slightly older than her father, a rumpled man with a half smile and a shaggy head of gray hair.

Nancy smiled. "When I told Dad about my research, he immediately suggested that I talk to you. I'm glad you were free for dinner this evening."

"An old bachelor like me will take any opportunity to sample Hannah Gruen's cooking," Tyrell said. He gallantly raised his glass to the Drews' housekeeper, who sat across the dining table.

"I just happened to remember your talking about the Delia Cox case," Carson Drew said to his friend. "You told me how surprised you were that when the estate was settled it turned out she left so little money, aside from the proceeds from the sale of the house."

Evan Tyrell nodded. "Right—it was strange, considering she had inherited the Sassoon fortune four years earlier. I wasn't the Sassoons' lawyer— that was Richard Beck; he's passed on now. But we all assumed Delia had become a wealthy woman after Sarah Sassoon died. She often complained that she had more money than she needed. I didn't know her very well, and she didn't hire me until after she inherited the money. Until then, of course, she'd never needed a lawyer."

"Maybe Miss Sassoon spent her entire fortune over the years," Hannah said, thinking out loud. "Those two women lived together in that huge house for a long time. They had taxes to pay, bills to take care of, servants to hire. . . ."

"I wonder how the Sassoon money was invested," Carson Drew mused. "Presumably it wasn't just sitting in a bank. If it was invested well, the two women should have been able to live on the interest. But maybe Sarah Sassoon owned real estate that was sold at the wrong time, or stocks that declined in value."

"Maybe there's something in that safe-deposit box I told you about," Nancy suggested to Delia's lawyer.

Evan Tyrell didn't look hopeful. "I'll go over the estate accounting to see if it's listed. If it isn't, I can draft some papers to petition the bank to open the box for us. But I'll need her nephew Roger's authorization first, and he's hard to get hold of. He lives out of town."

"Who is Roger?" Hannah asked. She placed a second wedge of lemon pie on his dessert plate, urging him to continue his story.

"Thank you so much," Tyrell said, eyeing the pie happily. He picked up his fork. "Roger? He's Delia's heir. I urged her to write a will, even though she didn't care what happened to the property after she died. She never felt it was rightfully hers. So I had to dig up her relatives for her. She'd been out of touch with her own family for years."

"And you unearthed this nephew," Nancy's father said.

"Her only relative," Tyrell said. "She'd met him once or twice, when he was a little boy, but he's in his forties now. They didn't really know each other, but blood is blood. She agreed that everything could go to him."

"A surprise inheritance—he must have been thrilled," Hannah said, clapping her hands.

Evan Tyrell sighed. " 'Thrilled' is not the word for it. As soon as he knew why we had contacted him, Roger showed up in River Heights. He was suddenly very solicitous of his old auntie, after all these years. They met a few times, but apparently it didn't go well."

Carson Drew stirred his coffee. "How do you know that?"

"Just a guess," Tyrell admitted. "But about then Delia got the notion to hire detectives to look for lost Sassoon relatives. I guessed it was because she felt she didn't deserve the Sassoon money. But maybe it was also because she didn't feel a bond with her own heir. She even asked me to draft a new will leaving everything to any Sassoons she found."

"Did you?" Nancy asked.

"I gave her a revised will, but she never signed it," Tyrell said. "Then her health began to fail, and she never hired the detective. It turned out all right in the end—Roger Cox told me he was reconciled with his aunt on her deathbed."

Nancy pursed her lips. "But she had already sold the house by then. Why did she do that?"

Tyrell shrugged. "I never figured that out. I was startled to hear she was selling it, in fact. She always said it was too big for her, but after all, it had been her home for over thirty years. I didn't handle the transaction; one of the real estate partners in my firm did. "

Nancy suddenly recalled the drawings she'd found in the storage closet in Haddon Hall. She couldn't admit how she had seen them, but maybe Mr. Tyrell knew about the project already. "Were there any plans to develop the Sassoon property in any other way—as a housing tract, for instance?" she asked.

"The Windridge suburbs have been booming lately," Carson Drew pointed out.

Tyrell shook his head. "I never heard of any such plans. I really doubt it. If there had been other offers, Delia wouldn't have sold the house to Carl Haddon as cheaply as she did." He savored one last bite of lemon pie.

"Maybe she just liked the idea of the place being a school," Nancy speculated.

Evan Tyrell lowered his shaggy eyebrows as he laid down his dessert fork. "That is possible. She did seem to be in a hurry to complete the sale. The school's old property was fire-damaged, and Haddon was desperate to relocate. She probably lowered the price to help him out. That's the kind of lady Delia was." The lawyer's eyes misted over. "Bless her soul."

Nancy felt her throat tighten with sympathy for Delia Cox. "It's too bad she never lived to see the place as a school," she said.

Tyrell sighed. "I agree. The building has been transformed, but at least it's full of youth and energy and life. She would have liked that."

Nancy pondered what Evan Tyrell had told her as she drove downtown the next morning. "Whose jacket was this, anyway—Sarah Sassoon's? Delia Cox's?" she murmured, shrugging her shoulders inside the satin jacket. "Whose key was in the pocket, and what does it unlock? And what is in that safe-deposit box?" She knew that, even with Evan Tyrell's help, it would take several days to get permission to open the box. It would be hard to wait that long.

She swerved into a left-turn lane, fretting at the Saturday traffic. The River Heights downtown shopping district had become more popular in the past couple of years. It was one-fifteen already, and she didn't want to be late for her appointment with the mysterious caller.

She lucked into a parking spot right across the street from La Parisienne, a trendy café on the corner of Main and Water Streets. Its tiny wicker tables were set outside on the warm spring day under a broad blue canopy, divided from the sidewalk by planters.

Nancy slid low in the driver's seat, staring across at the café. She hadn't yet decided whether she should actually meet with her anonymous friend or just spy on her. She'd get a look at the woman first. The caller said she'd be wearing a yellow hat. Nancy scanned the sidewalk, looking for a flash of yellow.

Then a young woman in a wide-brimmed yellow hat paused by the café entrance. Nancy sat up for a better look. The woman was of medium height and build, dressed in blue jeans and a navy windbreaker. The hat covered her hair, and her eyes were hidden behind sunglasses. She doesn't want to be recognized, Nancy thought. That tells me she's up to no good.

Nancy slid back down, using her sideview mirror to observe the woman. If she knows I drive a blue Mustang, Nancy thought, she might spot me here.

The woman in the yellow hat didn't look across the street. Leaning against the brass railing of the café entrance, she fidgeted and peered anxiously at the pedestrians, checking her watch repeatedly.

Ten minutes passed, then fifteen. Let's see how long she'll wait, Nancy thought. How important is this jacket to her?

At one fifty-five the woman straightened up, her fists clenched. She turned with a flounce of her elbows and strode away. Now's my chance, Nancy thought. She sprang out of her car and dashed off in the direction the woman had gone.

Following the yellow hat should have been easy, but weekend crowds clogged the sidewalks. Nancy bobbed and weaved her way among the strolling shoppers, jumping up to see over their heads, sprinting across an intersection to beat the red light. Her one advantage was that the woman didn't know she was being tailed. Nancy began to draw closer to her.

Suddenly a hand grabbed Nancy's arm. She spun around, startled. There stood Jack Ryman, the ponytailed secondhand dealer.

"Nancy Drew, right?" he said, lowering his head down to look at her over his wire-rims. "Your friend Bess Marvin called me yesterday."

Nancy tried to tug her arm away, but Ryman still held it. "Oh, did she?" she said, distracted by the thought of the yellow hat escaping.

"She wanted a list of all the stores I sold Sassoon stuff to," Ryman said. "Has she had any luck?"

"I don't know; she hasn't finished yet. But thanks for helping!" Nancy yanked her arm free.

"I was just curious—what are you looking for?" Ryman pressed on as Nancy started to back away from him. "Just in case I run across it myself."

"I can't talk now!" Nancy turned and then jogged away.

Behind her, she heard Ryman calling, "You know, a lot of people seem interested in the stuff I sold from that house. . . ."

Nancy darted frantically among the pedestrians and hurried to the next corner. The light was red.

Rising on tiptoe, she pivoted, searching in every direction for the yellow hat.

She had lost sight of it in the crowd.

Nancy slammed a fist against her thigh, furious. Now she would never know who that woman was or why she wanted the satin jacket! If only Jack Ryman hadn't come along . . .

Then a worrisome thought struck Nancy. Did Jack Ryman know she was chasing that woman—and had he stopped Nancy on purpose to let her get away?

7

Someone Is Watching

"So you think Jack Ryman is in cahoots with the woman in the yellow hat?" Bess asked that evening. She looked intrigued.

Nancy took a slice of pizza from the carton on the Marvins' kitchen table. "That would explain why he stopped me on the street this afternoon, acting like my best friend all of a sudden."

"It would also explain how the mystery woman learned that you had the jacket," George pointed out. She picked a piece of pepperoni off her slice. "He was pretty eager to get the key from you. Maybe he cooked up this scheme with a girlfriend to get the jacket away from you."

"But he wanted the key, not the jacket," Nancy said. "And he would have known that I'd never

61

leave the key in the jacket, even if I did sell it to a stranger."

"If he wanted the key, he should have found it before he sold it," Bess declared. She wiped pizza sauce off her chin with a paper napkin, frowning. "It wasn't until we showed up that he realized he might have sold something of value."

Nancy picked up her glass of soda. "That reminds me of another thing he said this afternoon. I was trying to get away from him at the time, so I didn't focus on what he was saying. But now it's coming back to me. He said that a lot of people seem to be interested in the Sassoon stuff. I wonder who else he means, besides us."

George raised her eyebrows. "Remember what he was saying on the phone the first time we visited him? 'It's out of my hands now.' Maybe someone was bugging him to locate an item from the estate, something he'd already sold."

"Ryman did sound testy, as if the person on the phone was being nasty," Bess recalled. She wrinkled her nose. "Maybe the caller was getting desperate."

"We do know possibly one other character who's looking for some Sassoon object," Nancy pointed out. "The intruder at the school may have been seeking something. It makes sense that he'd want something from the old estate and not from the school."

Bess's eyes darkened with concern. "Nan, you don't suppose Jack Ryman could've been the intruder, do you?"

Nancy shrugged, licking sauce off her fingers. "Why not?"

"But he already had access to all the Sassoon belongings," Bess argued. "Why would he need to break into the house?"

"Besides," George added, "if he thought the Sassoons had owned something of value, he'd have examined everything much more carefully. Remember, he overlooked that key in your jacket pocket."

Bess sipped her soda thoughtfully. "I just can't see Jack as a criminal. If he was trying to keep us from finding stuff, why did he draw up that list of antique stores for me? He was perfectly willing to do that when I asked him."

"And has the list been helpful?" Nancy asked.

Bess nodded. "Totally. I found several other Sassoon pieces. Let me show you." She hopped up from the table and fetched a stack of photos from the kitchen counter.

"You even took pictures—how efficient," George said.

"I knew you'd want to see these lovely antiques," Bess said. "I told the store owners I needed to show my decorator the photos before I bought anything." A shadow flickered over her face. "I

63

won't have to buy these things when I find them, will I, Nancy? I mean, antique furniture is expensive."

"Of course not, Bess," Nancy reassured her. "Just examine the pieces in the store. That should tell us whether we've found anything of interest."

"Well, none of them are outstandingly valuable," Bess said, spreading out her photos on the table. "They're good antiques, but they're not museum-quality—nothing that someone would scheme to own."

Her gaze drifted over the snapshots. "I love this tufted velvet sofa and love seat, though. They're a matching pair, but I found them in two different stores."

"What a shame! The set shouldn't have been broken up," George said.

"Well, this pair of maple rocking chairs was kept together," Bess said, pointing to another snapshot. "And so were this bed and nightstand."

"Oh, I love those sleigh beds," Nancy said. "Look at the carving on the headboard. What kind of wood is that?"

"Rosewood," Bess said. "Apparently it was very popular in the twenties. A lot of the Sassoon furniture dates from that period."

Nancy sighed. "I can just imagine what all this furniture looked like in that house. It must have been a showplace."

"I like this," George said, picking up a photo to study it closer. "A silver comb-and-brush set. What's that engraved on the back of the mirror?"

"A monogram—SAS, just like the ones on the linen blouses I bought from the Telltale Heart." Bess sighed. "Which, by the way, don't fit me. Sarah Sassoon must have been one of those willowy types—not like me." She pulled unhappily on a blond curl. "They might fit you, though, Nancy. Why don't you try one on?"

Nancy wiped her hands on a napkin. "You don't mind?"

Bess shook her head. "They're too pretty not to be worn. Besides, they really would go with your new jacket."

Nancy hopped up eagerly and followed Bess to her bedroom. The linen blouses were cut slim, with darts and tucks bringing them in close at the waist. The one Nancy tried on hung perfectly on her slender frame. She swiveled to check the back in Bess's bedroom mirror.

Bess thrust the second blouse into Nancy's hands. "Take them both," she declared. "Just promise you'll take good care of them."

George, sprawled on Bess's bed, giggled. "Yeah, Nan, don't wear them when you're chasing burglars through the woods and climbing stone walls, okay?"

Nancy grinned. "I promise."

The three girls returned to the kitchen to clean up their pizza dinner. "So, how many more antique stores do you have to check out?" Nancy asked Bess.

"Four more, plus another rare-book shop," Bess said. "Ooh, did I tell you I discovered the Sassoon family Bible at Past Times Books?"

Nancy's eyes lit up. "The family Bible?"

Bess beamed with delight. "Yes. Where's the photo?" She shuffled through the stack and produced a snapshot of a heavy leather-bound volume with gilded pages. Then she flipped to a second photo that showed a family tree, meticulously drawn on the book's front page. "There's her name, Sarah Amelia Sassoon," Bess said, pointing to one of the top branches of the tree. "An only child, apparently."

Nancy frowned and bent over the picture. "It looks as if there was something else written next to Sarah's name," she said. "But it was scratched out. See these faint lines?"

Bess peered at the photo. "You're right. Could it be a brother or sister who died as a baby?"

Nancy cocked her head. "Funny, Mr. Tyrell said something last night about long-lost Sassoon relatives. Maybe Delia knew something. Bess, is that store open tomorrow?"

Bess tried to remember. "I didn't notice."

"Because we should buy that book," Nancy declared. "It might help us find someone else who feels entitled to a piece of the Sassoon estate."

She tucked Bess's photos into her backpack, along with the pair of linen blouses. "I'll give these photos a closer look at home tonight. Maybe I'll spot something unusual about one of the pieces of furniture."

"Searching is hard when we don't know what we're looking for," George said, her hands in her jeans pockets.

"Well, whoever else is searching seems to know just what he's looking for," Nancy said wryly, swinging the backpack onto her shoulders. "And he seems to think it's pretty important. Who knows— maybe he'll lead us to it. If he starts feeling desperate, he may show his hand to us. Anyway, good night, guys. Talk to you tomorrow."

Nancy got in to her Mustang and headed for home. As she pulled onto her street, she looked toward her house to see if the lights were on. She'd been so preoccupied with her mystery that she had no idea what her father and Hannah had planned for this evening. "I did call and tell Hannah not to expect me home for dinner, didn't I?" she murmured guiltily.

One light burned at the back of the house— Nancy couldn't tell if it was from the kitchen or from Hannah's bedroom. The front windows were dark, and even the porch light was off. Nancy guessed that her father was out somewhere and Hannah had turned in early.

Just then a shadow darted along a row of shrubbery underneath the living room windows. Nancy's grip tightened on the steering wheel, and she slowed down her car. She peered ahead at the mass of shifting shadows in the yard.

The dark shape moved again. Nancy saw the outline of someone's head, rising level with the living room windowsill.

Someone was hiding in the shrubbery, spying on Nancy's house!

8

On Closer Look

Had the intruder in the yard spotted Nancy's car yet? She had no idea, but in case he hadn't, she switched off the engine. The quieter her approach, the better. She flipped off her headlights, too, and coasted along the street in the dark.

Peering ahead, Nancy saw the huddled shape shift slowly, moving along the first-floor windows. Nancy wondered if he was planning to break in or just watching the people inside. She had a sickening feeling that if he was spying, she was the one he wanted to spy on.

I've got to take him by surprise, she thought. She would learn nothing by scaring him off; she needed to know who was stalking her and what he wanted.

With a soft whisper of tires on pavement, the Mustang rolled forward. Nancy held her breath and searched the darkness ahead as she neared the foot of her driveway.

Suddenly a blaze of light switched on above the front door. Startled, the intruder reared up from his hiding place in the bushes. He spun around and recklessly crashed out of the cover of the shrubbery. Still crouching low, he dashed across an open stretch of lawn and plunged into the narrow side yard.

"Hannah!" Nancy groaned. "What a time to turn on the front light!"

She swerved her car into the driveway, yanked on the parking brake, and jumped out. A sense of urgency filled her with energy. She bolted at top speed around the corner of her house, following in the intruder's wake.

Yellow lamplight spilling from the windows softly illuminated the yard. Rounding a back corner of the house, Nancy saw a figure in black rushing toward the high fence. From the person's height and build, Nancy couldn't even be sure if it was a man or a woman. But she did recognize the hooded sweatshirt and black ski mask.

I met you the other night—at Haddon Hall, Nancy thought grimly. She ran madly in pursuit.

The intruder grasped the bar at the top of the fence and, with a powerful swing, vaulted to the top. Nancy flung herself against the fence and scrambled upward. She strained to grab the dark sneakers just above her head.

Without a moment's hesitation, the intruder launched himself into the neighbors' yard. Nancy could hear an urgent thrashing as he fought his way through the shrubbery there.

Nancy hauled herself to the top of the fence. The neighboring yard was dark and thickly planted; no lights were on at the house. Nancy yelled for help even though she felt pretty sure her neighbor wasn't home.

Then, on the street beyond the neighbors' house, Nancy saw the figure in black sprinting through a pool of harsh yellow light thrown down by a streetlamp. With pounding footsteps the intruder took off up the street.

Nancy hit the ground, but by the time she reached the street, the intruder had vanished from sight.

Nancy sank down on the curb to catch her breath. She swallowed hard, choking back her disappointment. "Think clearly," she scolded herself. "Why would the Haddon Hall intruder—whoever it is—stake out our house? Just to watch what I was doing?"

Then it dawned on her. Nancy felt her scalp prickle.

He must want the brass key she'd found in the satin pocket of her jacket.

71

Nancy set her jaw stubbornly. "Well, he didn't get it, and he can't have it," she muttered to herself. She jumped to her feet and threaded her way through various backyards to her house.

Hannah was sitting at the kitchen table when Nancy came in the back door. The housekeeper's kindly face was creased with concern. "I saw your car parked at a crazy angle out in front," she said, rising to her feet when she saw Nancy. "I heard someone running through the yard, and I thought I heard you shouting. Nancy, what's going on?"

"Everything's okay, Hannah," Nancy reassured her, slipping an arm around the older woman's shoulders. "I saw someone in the front yard, peeping through our windows. I ran him off the property."

Hannah looked worried. "Peeping in our windows?"

"It was probably just some neighborhood kid," Nancy said, hoping to get Hannah's mind off the incident. "When you turned on the porch light, he got scared and took off."

Nancy began to head upstairs to her bedroom. Her mind was focused on that brass key. She wouldn't relax until she was sure it was right where she had left it.

"Does this have something to do with the case you're working on?" Hannah asked, following Nancy to the front hall.

Nancy shrugged. "Maybe," she admitted. "But the important thing is that no one's been hurt and nothing's been stolen." She trotted up the stairs, Hannah following her.

"I don't think he'll come back," Nancy said brightly over her shoulder, "now that he knows I've seen him. We'll just be sure to lock the doors tonight."

"We lock the doors every night," Hannah replied. "I'll feel better when your father gets home."

"Me, too," Nancy agreed.

She hurried into her bedroom, heading straight for the jewelry case on her dresser. When she first put the key here, she'd only been concerned that she wouldn't misplace it. Now she realized it was not a safe hiding place. What could be more obvious? The case didn't even have a lock on it.

She lifted the leather lid and looked inside. The brass key still lay there on the purple velvet lining. It was nestled between a chunky bead bracelet and a silver locket that had belonged to Nancy's mother.

Nancy breathed a sigh of relief. She picked up the key and held it tight.

Then she spied a plain silver chain, lying in a puddle in the bottom of the case. She pulled it out and threaded it through the hole in the top of the key. She fastened the chain around her neck and let the key hang like a pendant against her chest.

"Anyone who wants this key will have to get past me," she said out loud to herself. "Next thing you know, I'll be renting a safe-deposit box for this safe-deposit-box key."

Hannah was still lingering in the hallway when Nancy came out. "What about your car, Nan? You left it blocking the driveway so that your father won't be able to get past it."

"I'm going out now to move it into the garage," Nancy promised. "I left my backpack in the car, anyway. There's something in it that I want to show you."

Hannah insisted on standing on the front steps, watching, until Nancy had safely put her car in the garage. Once they were both inside again, Hannah locked the front door firmly. "Your father's got his own key," she pointed out. "He can let himself in when he comes home."

"Sit down, Hannah, and look at what I've got," Nancy said. The sooner she could get Hannah's mind off the intruder, the better. "Bess bought these at that same vintage-clothing boutique where I got my jacket. Aren't they cool?"

She pulled the linen blouses out of her backpack. Hannah took them in her capable hands and bent over them with interest.

"My goodness, these are lovely," she said in an admiring voice. She gently stroked the fabric. "It's a very fine linen, isn't it? And the monogram has been stitched by hand. Expert needlework, using silk embroidery floss." She looked up at Nancy with a flash of humor. "Not like the clumsy stitching inside that satin pocket in your jacket. Remember?"

Nancy smiled. "These will go great with the jacket, though, won't they?"

"I thought you said that Bess bought them."

"She did, but they're a little tight on her, so she let me have them," Nancy explained.

Hannah chuckled. "Poor Bess. I suppose this has convinced her she needs to start another diet."

"Which won't last more than a day," Nancy added ruefully. "You know Bess."

Looking back at the two blouses she held, Hannah raised an eyebrow. "That's strange."

Nancy perked up. "What?"

Hannah stepped over to spread the blouses on the nearest table, side by side. She switched on the lamp above them. "Look at the initial on this side," Hannah said, pointing to the silken embroidery on the right-hand blouse. "This right-hand letter. It stands for the owner's middle name, right?"

Nancy nodded. "It's an *A*. Sarah Sassoon's middle name was Amelia."

"Then what does this stand for?" Hannah wondered, pointing at the second monogram.

Nancy leaned forward and stared at the pale-blue curlicued letters. "I thought it was an *A,* too."

"It isn't," Hannah said crisply. She traced the letter with her finger. "See—the two side lines don't meet at the top. In this curvy script, they do look similar. But this is an *H*. No doubt about it."

Nancy frowned, puzzled. "Do you suppose the embroiderer made a mistake?"

Hannah looked skeptical. "The whole point of having a monogram is to wear your own initials. If the monogram's wrong, you send it back to be fixed, or you throw it away. You certainly don't preserve the blouse for decades."

"You mean—"

Hannah crossed her arms and nodded. "I'll bet this wasn't Sarah Sassoon's blouse."

Nancy gazed at the blouses, thunderstruck. "Then whose was it?"

9

Family Secrets

"But the two blouses match so perfectly," Nancy said, frowning. "It can't be just a coincidence."

"Oh, they were made as a pair, that's for sure," Hannah declared. She studied the two linen blouses spread before them on the table. "But for two people, not one. This second person had the initials S.H.S. Could there have been another Sassoon sister?"

Nancy chewed her lip. "The family Bible showed that Sarah was an only child . . . unless—"

Nancy hurried over to her backpack and dug out the snapshot of the Sassoon family tree Bess had found in their family Bible. She held it up to the light to study the faint scratch marks next to Sarah's name.

"I'd have to see this page in person to be sure," she said, thinking out loud. "But a name could definitely have been deleted here." She looked up eagerly at Hannah. "Bess thought it might have been a baby who died in infancy."

Hannah shook her head. "It would have to be a sister who lived to be a grown-up," she pointed out. "This is an adult-size blouse. A twin, maybe, if they wore matching clothes."

Nancy's eyes sparkled. "Sarah Sassoon's will said she had no living relatives," she recalled, "but what if she was wrong?"

Hannah folded her arms. "The sister may well have died by then," she said. "After all, these blouses date from the forties, which was a long time ago. Sarah's sister may have lived to be an adult, but not to become elderly. How old was Sarah when she died?"

"She was seventy-two," Nancy recalled from the probate records. "But even if her sister died first, if she had children, they would be Sarah's relatives, too."

Hannah cupped her chin on one hand. "I guess the big question is, why was this sister's name scratched out of the family Bible?"

"Maybe she died tragically at a young age, and Sarah, in her grief, scratched her name out," Nancy speculated.

"Which gets us back to Sarah not having any living relatives," Hannah reasoned.

"Unless the sister had children," Nancy reminded her.

Hannah smiled. "You're not giving up on that possibility, are you?"

"No, I'm not," Nancy declared. "Delia Cox thought there might be long-lost Sassoon relatives somewhere. She must have known something. Why else would she have planned to hire a detective to hunt for them?"

"Well, I guess she *has* hired a detective." Hannah chuckled. "From beyond the grave, she's hired you!"

Sunday dawned crisp and clear, a beautiful day. River Heights still lay cocooned in its Sunday morning quiet as Nancy, Bess, and George pulled up in front of Past Times Books.

The store stood on a side street that was closed to car traffic, to encourage pedestrians to stroll and shop. This morning, though, all the neighboring shops were still closed. Past Times's bay window hung over the sidewalk, with a clutter of intriguing books inside. Bess pressed her nose against the glass. "See, they've got almost the entire series of Wizard of Oz books," she pointed out. "Those are pretty rare. The illustrations in them are amazing."

"You're getting very knowledgeable about this stuff, Bess," George commented.

Bess smiled. "Thanks to all the time I'm spending in antique stores. Owners love to show their special collections to interested customers. Sometimes I wonder how they can ever bear to sell them."

Nancy studied the store hours painted on the front-door glass. "It *is* open on Sunday," she said happily. "It opens at noon." She checked her watch. "That's ten minutes away. Let's just wait here."

Bess leaned against the windowsill, looking up and down the street. "Do you see a drugstore or grocery open nearby? I could use a can of diet soda. My stomach's rumbling."

George rolled her eyes. "I keep telling you, Bess, you've got to eat breakfast even when you're trying to lose weight. Without it you just make yourself hungry and weak, and then you break down and eat everything in sight."

Bess looked hurt. "It's easy for you to preach, George," she complained. "You never need to go on a diet."

"That's right, because I exercise," George said.

"Bess doesn't *need* to go on a diet either," Nancy put in. "You look good the way you are, Bess. Believe me."

The girls continued to chat as they waited outside the shop. They paused when bells chimed from a church tower a few blocks away. They silently counted the strokes together. "Twelve," George said with satisfaction. "Now it'll open up."

Nancy looked up and down the street. "Well, I don't see the owner," she said. "He has to come to unlock the door."

"I think the owner's a she," Bess said. "The woman who showed me the Oz books yesterday acted as if this was her store."

George shaded her eyes and peered into the darkened shop. "She'll have to turn the lights on, too, and open up the cash register. It always takes a few minutes to get ready for business."

Nancy shrugged. "Well, independent shop owners don't always keep strict hours. She'll be here soon, I'm sure."

Ten minutes crawled by, then fifteen. The girls tried to avoid looking at their watches, but they began to feel restless.

At last they heard footsteps on the sidewalk, coming around the corner. All three perked up and stared expectantly in that direction.

To their surprise, Jack Ryman came into sight, dressed in his usual worn jeans and cowboy boots. In his arms he lugged a large and obviously heavy cardboard carton.

"Mr. Ryman!" Bess called out.

Ryman grinned over the top of the box. "Hey,

Bess!" he answered. "Nancy, too. Did you get to where you were going in such a hurry yesterday?"

"Yes," Nancy replied. She was wary of telling the secondhand dealer too much.

"What do you have in the box?" Bess asked as Ryman reached them.

With a slight groan, he stopped and set the box down on the sidewalk. "Books," he said. "I cleaned up at a church rummage sale yesterday. I was hoping to sell them to Jane Jacoby, the woman who runs Past Times. What are you three waiting for?"

"Bess told us this was a good store," Nancy said. "We're here to do some book shopping."

"Glad I turned you on to it," Ryman said with a friendly grin. "Isn't it open?"

"Not yet," George said. "We figure she's running late."

Ryman looked puzzled. "Really? That's not like Jane. She's usually very punctual, a good business-woman and a true book lover. It's a pleasure doing business with her."

Nancy met Ryman's glance with a smile, but her mind was whirling. Was it a coincidence that Ryman had popped up again? Or had he known the girls would be there?

"I'm surprised to see you working on a Sunday," she said casually.

Jack Ryman shrugged. "In my business there are no hours. I bought these books yesterday, and they were weighing down the trunk of my car. I thought, why haul them upstairs and store them when I could sell them today?" He paused. "But if Jane's not here, maybe I'll come back tomorrow."

Nancy and George traded quizzical glances over his back as he bent to pick up the heavy carton.

"Should we tell her you were here?" Bess asked.

"Don't worry about it," Ryman said. "Well, I'll see you around. Happy shopping, girls." He turned and toted the box back the way he had come.

Nancy said nothing until he had turned the corner and was out of earshot. "Don't you think that was weird?" she said.

"He carried that heavy box here and then barely waited two minutes before he gave up and left," George said.

"I wonder if he really had books in there," Nancy mused. "Did anyone see inside?"

The other two shook their heads. "Maybe he *is* following you, Nancy," George said. "But why?"

"He must know the Sassoon family Bible is in this store," Nancy said. "Maybe he wants to keep us from reading it."

"Then why did he leave?" George wondered. "If he wanted to stop us, he'd have waited with us and followed us into the store."

"Besides, he was the one who sent me here to find Sassoon books," Bess argued. "Why tell me that if he didn't want us to read the Bible?"

Just then they heard a car gun its engine around the corner where Ryman had just disappeared. The three girls looked up, curious.

A gray sedan bolted suddenly out of the cross street, hurtling across the intersection.

"That's the car!" George exclaimed. "I'm sure that's the car we saw drive away from Haddon Hall the night you chased the burglar, Nancy."

Nancy stared after it, trying to impress its image on her memory. "Did anyone get a look at the license plates?"

"Too far away." Bess sighed. "Do you think it's Jack Ryman's car? He was just here, after all."

"Why would he have out-of-state plates?" George asked. "I couldn't read the numbers, but I saw the color. Those are not local plates."

The girls continued to discuss the case as they waited impatiently. The nearby clock tower had just struck one o'clock when they finally saw Jane Jacoby walk up the street. She was a perky-looking woman with short reddish hair, horn-rimmed glasses, and multilayered dark clothes.

Seeing the girls, she waved apologetically. "Sorry I'm late!" she called out, hurrying the last few yards. A big ring of keys jingled in her hand.

"I hope you haven't been waiting too long," she chattered as she unlocked the front door. "A customer called me at home last night with a special request—you know how people are. She'd just found out I had this certain volume, and she had to get her hands on it immediately. For some reason she couldn't drive into town to pick it up herself, so I drove it out to her this morning."

"That was nice of you," Bess remarked.

Jane Jacoby replied with a silvery laugh. "Well, I'm a sucker for helping people get matched up with books they treasure."

She pushed the door open and hurried into the dusky store, snapping on lights as she went. "Look around, look around," she invited the girls with an airy wave of her hand. She trotted over to the long wooden sales counter in the back of the store.

Though small, Past Times used every possible inch of its space to display books. Tall shelves divided the room into several book-lined crannies. Nancy saw Bess pop into a side alcove. She and George followed.

Bess was down on her knees, scrabbling through a bottom shelf full of thick, dusty volumes. "It isn't here!" she wailed softly.

"What are you looking for?" Jane Jacoby poked her head around the tall shelves.

"A Bible," Bess replied, looking up. "I saw it here yesterday. A huge old Bible with fancy gilded letters and inset pictures on the front cover."

Jane Jacoby sighed. "Oh, yes, I know the one you mean. It's a beautiful volume."

"So where is it?" Bess asked.

"This is such a coincidence." Jacoby put her hands on her hips. "That just happens to be the book I took out to the urgent customer this morning. To the headmistress of that new school, Haddon Hall. Vanessa Chilton."

10

Nobody's Talking

Nancy and Bess looked at each other in alarm. "Haddon Hall?" Bess gasped.

"Vanessa Chilton?" Nancy added.

"Isn't that a pity," the bookstore owner said. "I had that book here for almost three months and nobody noticed it. Then I got two interested customers at once. I hate to see a book lover disappointed. I do have other illustrated Bibles. Or was it the ornate cover you were attracted to?"

Bess scrambled to her feet. "Uh, the cover—I need something exactly that color and that size. There's nothing else here like it. Well, we'd better go."

Jane Jacoby looked puzzled when the three girls scurried out of the bookshop.

"She must think we're nuts," Nancy said once they hit the street. "After waiting so long, we raced out of there so quickly."

"I wonder how Ms. Chilton found out that Past Times had the Sassoon family Bible," George remarked, breaking into a jog.

"The same way we did, I'll bet," Nancy said grimly. "From Jack Ryman."

Piling into the Mustang, the three girls headed north for Haddon Hall. "What are you going to say to Ms. Chilton, Nancy?" Bess wondered as they swung onto Windridge Road. "Are you going to ask her to sell you the book?"

"I hardly think she'd sell it," George said. "Not after she begged Jane Jacoby to go to all that trouble to deliver it to her."

"She sounded as if she was in an awful hurry to get it," Nancy said, tapping thoughtfully on the steering wheel. "I wonder if she knew we were after it, too."

George gazed out the window as the woods began to close in around them. "Do you think she didn't want it for herself—she just wanted to keep *us* from seeing it?"

"Maybe a little of both," Nancy said. She paused to giggle as the car bounced over the little humpbacked bridge. "Ticklebelly Bridge," she announced.

"Whoa!" Bess said from the backseat. "That was fun."

Nancy swung the car around the sharp curve. "To be honest, I don't know what I should say to Ms. Chilton," she admitted. "I don't need to buy that Bible from her, but I'd love to examine it closely. I have no idea how to talk her into letting me see it, though. She's really on her guard against me."

"How do you think Vanessa Chilton figures into all this?" Bess asked Nancy. "I mean, we know she isn't the intruder you saw those two times. She wouldn't have been trying to break into her own school."

"Don't rule her out," Nancy warned as they approached Haddon Hall's front gates. "It does sound perverse, I agree. But remember, she doesn't own the school—she's just a hired headmistress. That could explain why she refused to call in the police to investigate the break-ins."

As Nancy swung into the drive, she had to step suddenly on the brake. The iron gates were pulled shut across the drive. "That's a change," Nancy said, surprised.

"They *have* had two break-ins," George said. "Looks like they've beefed up security since Thursday night."

Nancy spotted a chrome panel freshly installed on the left-hand stone pillar. She rolled down her window to study it. The round glass eye of a small video camera squinted at her.

"This is new also," she said.

"How does it work?" George asked.

Nancy stretched her arm out the window and pressed a square black button labeled Talk. A speaker below it squawked briefly, then a staticky voice demanded, "Who is it?"

Nancy cleared her throat and faced the camera squarely. "My name is Nancy Drew. I'm here to speak to Ms. Chilton."

"Okay," the voice squawked back. Nancy heard a buzz, then an iron click. With a mechanical grinding noise, the gates began to swing open. Nancy moved her foot toward the accelerator.

Then the gates stopped with a sudden jolt, still only a few inches apart. The chrome panel squawked again: a different voice—gruffer and more gravelly. "Today is Sunday. Ms. Chilton doesn't have appointments on Sunday."

Nancy recognized Vernon's voice. She tightened her grip on the steering wheel in frustration. "The bookstore owner, Jane Jacoby, asked me to come," she improvised. "There was something about that book she sold Ms. Chilton this morning . . ."

"Wait a minute," Vernon growled back. There was a long silence. Nancy traded tense looks with her friends.

"I don't suppose we could ram down those gates, could we?" George suggested softly.

"They look pretty strong," Nancy said, eyeing the heavy iron palings. "Besides, it would cause more trouble than it's worth. We might get through the gates, but then what?"

The speaker squawked again. "Ms. Chilton says she is not to be disturbed," Vernon announced. "Please phone her office tomorrow and make an appointment. Goodbye."

Nancy blew out a deep breath of frustration. She shoved the gearshift lever into Reverse and grudgingly backed her car away from the gates.

"We'll never get a look at that Bible now," Bess complained.

"She sure seems determined to keep you out," George commented.

Glumly Nancy steered the car onto Windridge Road and headed back toward town.

"I wonder what Ms. Chilton's up to," George mused. "What's her deep, dark reason for refusing to talk to you?"

"She's thinks Nancy's a reporter," Bess said. "And she's still trying to cover up those fishy break-ins."

Nancy shook her head. "Worse, she thinks *I'm* the intruder, remember? And now she knows I'm after that Bible as well. Frankly, I don't blame her for not wanting me on the school grounds. But it's sure going to make solving this mystery a lot harder."

"So, where do we go next?" George asked.

Nancy narrowed her eyes, focusing on the road ahead. "I'm getting more and more curious about

Jack Ryman," she said slowly. "What role is he playing in all this?"

"He seems friendly enough," Bess said.

"Yeah, so friendly he pops up everywhere we go," George pointed out.

"But he's helping us. He told us where to find the stuff he sold," Bess argued.

"And he's apparently telling other people, too," Nancy said. "Well, we know he's working today, even though it's Sunday, right? So how about we pay him a little visit?"

The bright spring sky began to cloud over as the girls drove back into River Heights. Under a leaden sky, the building by the river appeared gloomier and more run-down than ever. Nancy pulled up across the street, eyeing the top-floor windows. "No lights are on up there," she noted.

"Maybe he just didn't turn them on," Bess said. "If there's enough light coming through the windows . . ."

"Those windows are filthy, and half of them are blocked by shelves," George reminded her. "He couldn't see to work in there without lights on."

"Let's go up anyway," Nancy said thoughtfully. "So what if he's not in the office? Sometimes you can learn more about someone when he's not around."

Bess leaned over the front seat. "You mean, we're going to break in, Nancy?"

"No, but we are going to see if a door might have been left open. There are no other people working in that building—no one to observe us going in or out. So, it's a perfect opportunity."

"What do you hope to find if we get in?" George asked Nancy.

"Just think—if we could find an inventory of the things he sold from the Sassoon estate," Nancy said. "Or a message on his phone machine, telling us who else is hunting for those items or if he's working with an accomplice."

"Like Vanessa Chilton, for instance?" Bess raised her eyebrows.

The girls paused, looking at one another.

"Let's try!" George declared.

They jumped out of the car and paused on the curb, looking both ways for traffic on the deserted downtown street.

Then, with a whistling sound, something flew by Nancy's right temple. She crouched instinctively and threw her hands over her head.

Behind her she heard a heavy thud, followed by the sound of splintering glass. Nancy wheeled around. She gasped.

A brick had bounced off the hood of her Mustang after shattering the windshield in a sprawling web of cracks.

11

Danger Closes In

"That brick didn't fall by accident," Nancy spluttered, clenching her fists.

She spun around, searching the blank building fronts on both sides of the street. There were no open windows. There were no cars parked nearby. There didn't seem to be a soul in sight.

"You guys okay?" Nancy asked Bess and George.

They nodded. "That came awfully cl-cl-close, Nancy," Bess stammered. "It was aimed right at your head!"

"It looked that way, didn't it?" Nancy said grimly.

George pointed a shaky finger toward the brick. "Nancy, look. There's something attached to the brick with a rubber band."

Nancy sprang over to the car and picked up the

brick. She unwrapped a scrap of thick white paper that looked as if it had been torn from a bag. On it someone had scrawled a warning: "Beat it, Nancy Drew."

"Well, whoever threw this knows my name," Nancy reported. She folded the paper carefully. It could be useful evidence.

George tipped her head back to study the roofline of the buildings lining the street. "It must have come from high up, Nan," she said. "Someone could have thrown it from one of the roofs. But the street's so narrow that I can't say which side."

"Which means it could have been tossed from the roof of Jack Ryman's building," Bess added reluctantly. "But that doesn't necessarily prove it was Ryman."

George shrugged. "He does look like a suspect, though. This is his neighborhood. Even if the brick came from another roof, we know Ryman is familiar with the turf. And we've already had one encounter with him today."

Nancy raised her eyebrows. "There are several different possibilities. Ryman could be tailing us— or he could be nervous because we're tailing him. Or somebody else could have followed us here."

"Or somebody else could be tailing Ryman, and maybe that person got spooked when we showed up," Bess suggested.

Nancy sighed. "Well, whoever threw the brick has had plenty of time to get away, so we aren't likely to find out who it was. But I can tell you one thing"—Nancy's blue eyes glinted fiercely—"this makes me more determined than ever to solve this case. Someone is clearly searching for some item from the Sassoon mansion. Maybe it's that key I found; maybe it's something else. But someone is starting to get impatient."

"And dangerous." George frowned.

"Whoever it is must be after something valuable," Bess declared. Nancy nodded. "I agree. I'm afraid our friend will stop at nothing to get it. Which just means we'll have to find what he's searching for first."

The next morning, Monday, Bess drove up to an auto repair shop in Nancy's neighborhood. Nancy was waiting outside. She waved when Bess pulled over.

Bess leaned over to pop open the passenger door. "You're not wearing your new jacket today," she noticed.

Nancy smiled as she slid into the passenger seat. "The air is too chilly. Besides, the person we're chasing is starting to play rough. I don't want that antique jacket to get stained or torn."

Bess nodded. "How long before they'll have your car fixed?" she asked.

"A couple of days," Nancy said. "They didn't have a windshield in stock and had to order one."

"That's a pain." Bess grimaced.

"Well, what can I do?" Nancy asked with a philosophical shrug. "In the meantime we've got plenty to do."

Bess pulled away from the curb. "George called me and said to pick her up downtown at Midstate. What's she up to?"

"I gave her the brass key this morning," Nancy explained. "We're hoping that Margo, the clerk she talked to before, can identify it as a key to one of their safe-deposit boxes. If it is, we can stop hunting for the lock that it fits."

Bess's eyes lit up. "Maybe Margo will let George open the box!"

Nancy shook her head. "I doubt it. That would be completely against bank regulations. They're not supposed to open a safe-deposit box for anyone but the owner."

"How do they know every owner?" Bess wondered.

"Well, you have to use your key. And they make you sign a register," Nancy said. "Your signature must match the one they've got on file. Besides, the clerk already knows that George isn't Delia Cox. The woman was helpful last Friday, but I don't think she could be *that* helpful."

"True, we don't want to make her lose her job," Bess realized.

"No one can open a deposit box for an unauthorized person," Nancy said. "Even Mr. Tyrell couldn't open one without the right forms and affidavits. In this case that would include approval from Delia's nephew."

"Maybe he can open it for us soon," Bess said optimistically.

"Don't hold your breath," Nancy replied. "We don't even know for sure that the key is to that safe-deposit box. Also, the legal details will take a long time."

"We can't afford to wait a long time," Bess said. "Our rival sure isn't going to wait."

Nancy added, "And until he finds what he's looking for, things could get more and more dangerous for us."

They spotted George in front of the bank, leaning against a carved stone handrail on the broad front steps. She waved and hurried forward when she recognized Bess's car.

"What did you find out?" Nancy asked eagerly as George climbed into the backseat.

George scrunched up her face in disappointment. "Nothing, absolutely nothing. My friend Margo seems to have had a personality change since last Friday. It was actually kind of weird."

"Didn't she remember you?" Bess asked, guiding the car into traffic.

"Oh, she recognized me all right," George said. "As soon as she saw me, she got all pale and flustered. She clammed up completely."

"Maybe she got in trouble after you left on Friday," Bess said. "You know, she did share privileged information with you."

Nancy nodded. "I was surprised she showed you the sign-in log and everything."

"Well, she didn't show me anything today," George said. "She threw me out, basically. She said if I didn't have an account there, I'd have to leave the vault area. So I did."

Looking out the window, Nancy spied the café where her anonymous caller had waited on Saturday. "There it is—La Parisienne," she said, half to herself.

Bess braked and swerved the car toward the curb. "Should I stop?"

"Why? The woman in the yellow hat is gone by now," George protested.

"Well, we have to go *somewhere* for lunch," Bess said. "We need to rethink our strategy, now that we've lost our bank connection."

Nancy smiled. "We can have lunch here if you want to, Bess. This café is supposed to be good."

Bess parked the car, and the three girls climbed out. It was still early, before the lunchtime rush.

They were quickly shown to an outdoor table, divided from the sidewalk only by a planter.

"So you didn't have a chance to show Margo the key?" Nancy asked George as they studied their menus.

George made a face. "That was weird, too. I showed her the key, hoping that would change her mind. As if having a key to one of the boxes would give me a right to be there. Well, she stared at that key as if it were red-hot. She couldn't take her eyes off it. She actually tried to swipe it from me."

Nancy leaned forward in her chair. "You're kidding!"

"I do not lie." George nodded solemnly. "I snatched it back, of course. But then she tried to talk me into giving it to her—she said it was bank property and she had to confiscate it. I refused to give it to her, but at least we know now that it's the key to a safe-deposit box and probably for that bank." She pulled the key from her pocket and handed it to Nancy. "You'd better hang on to it for safekeeping."

Taking the key, Nancy tapped it against her lips, thinking. "When you saw Margo on Friday, she was under the impression that Miss Cox was still alive. Did you ever tell her that Delia had died?"

George shook her head.

"So for all she knows, Delia could have given you the key to check on her box, right?"

"I guess so."

"The salads here sound delicious," Bess commented, lowering her menu.

"It's a pretty place," Nancy said, looking around. "I'm glad we stopped."

"It's nice being right on the street. I love to people-watch," George said, scanning the street. She suddenly stiffened. "Guys, look!"

Nancy twisted around to follow the direction of George's gaze. "What is it?"

George nodded toward the street. "There's that gray car again, heading toward us in the southbound lane."

Glancing at the car cruising down Water Street, Nancy recognized the sedan they'd seen the day before near Past Times Books. "Now's our chance to read the license plate. With all the traffic here, it can't speed away this time."

"Bess!" George hissed. "Sit down! Don't be so obvious. We don't want him to see us."

Bess had half-risen from her chair to gawk over the planter. With George yanking on her sleeve, she plopped back into her chair. "Well, if you want to see, you've got to look," she protested. She picked up a fork and began to play with a tub of butter on the table.

Nancy ducked down and craned her neck to glimpse the car between the clumps of flowers in the planter. Just then the traffic surged ahead. A small van cut in front of the gray car. Nancy groaned and crouched lower.

The van moved forward with a jerk and a screech. The gray car came into view again.

Nancy heard George gasp. "That girl in the car—" she burst out.

Nancy's eyes flew to the car window nearest them, the passenger side. She took in a swift glimpse of sunglasses and curly brown hair. Something familiar . . .

Then she felt George jump to her feet. "Margo!" George shouted, waving.

The driver of the car immediately gunned his engine, swerved recklessly around the van in front of him, and roared away, running a red light.

Nancy turned to George. "Nancy, that was my bank employee, Margo Rosnick," George said breathlessly.

Nancy drew a deep breath and stared in the wake of the mysterious gray car. "Not only that," she added. "That woman was also my anonymous caller!"

12

A New Suspect

"The woman in the yellow hat?" George asked Nancy, incredulous. "In that gray car? Are you sure?"

Nancy nodded. "Her hair was covered on Saturday, but she wore the same sunglasses. And the shape of her face was the same, I'm certain."

Bess raised a good point. "Nancy, you don't know that the girl you saw here on Saturday was the one who called you. You never talked to her, did you?"

"No," Nancy admitted. "But the girl in the yellow hat was Margo. And if Jack Ryman prevented me from following her, then she must be working with him. Which makes me think that gray car is his."

George slammed a fist into her palm. "I wish I'd seen that license plate. Did you, Nancy?"

Nancy blew out a breath of frustration. "No—it was too low."

"That's why you should have stood up," Bess said.

Nancy looked at her. "You mean . . . ?"

Bess nodded and pointed with her fork at the tub of butter. "I didn't have anything else to write it down with, so I marked it in here."

Nancy glanced at the gleaming yellow butter. Bess had used her fork to scrape a series of numbers into the surface: M68 7FOB. "It was a Nevada plate," Bess added.

Nancy broke into a grin. "Bess Marvin, I love you!" She jumped up and hugged her friend around the shoulders. Then she took a pen and notepad from her backpack and jotted the numbers down. "Let me find a phone and call Chief McGinnis," she said, excusing herself. "Order a cheese omelet for me if the waiter comes."

By the time Nancy had made her call and returned to the table, their food had arrived. As the girls ate, they discussed the significance of this latest information. "So chances are that it was Margo who called you wanting to buy your coat," George said to Nancy. "She was hoping to get the key from the pocket, no doubt."

"And after she failed on Saturday, she tried to

grab it this morning," Nancy agreed. "That makes it seem very likely that Margo was my caller and that she's after the key."

"How did she learn that you had the key in the first place?" Bess wondered.

"Had to be from Jack Ryman," George said. "He's the only person we told about the key."

Bess shook her head. "That car has Nevada plates. Jack isn't from Nevada; he's from River Heights. That can't be his car."

"He still could be part of the scheme," George argued.

Nancy picked at the cheese filling of her omelet, thinking. "We can't jump to conclusions. We saw Margo in the gray car, but that doesn't prove she's part of the scheme. Suppose our culprit just met her and is driving her around to pump her for information?"

George frowned. "He just met her? That explains why she wouldn't talk to me today, after being so friendly and helpful last Friday."

"Unless she was friendly on Friday on purpose," Nancy pointed out. "If she was already part of the scheme, she'd try to get information out of you. Was that how she learned that I'd bought a jacket with a key in the pocket?"

"I didn't tell her about the jacket—I only showed her the receipt," George declared. "And I didn't say where I'd gotten it."

Their waiter appeared beside the table. "Is one of you Nancy Drew?" he asked.

Nancy looked up sharply. "Who wants to know?"

"You've got a telephone call," the waiter replied.

"I'll be right back," Nancy promised her friends. She hurried to the maître d's desk, near the entrance.

Chief McGinnis was on the line. "I've got that license ID you wanted, Nancy," he said. "That car is registered in the name of Roger Cox."

"Delia's nephew!" Nancy exclaimed softly.

"You know this guy?" the police chief asked.

"I know who he is," Nancy replied.

"Is he harassing you? Want me to send an officer so you can make a formal complaint?"

"I have nothing to accuse Roger Cox of," Nancy admitted. "Driving around town is no crime. It's just that he happens to drive past us at suspicious times."

"Well, don't take any risks," Chief McGinnis warned Nancy. "Call me if you need help."

Nancy thanked the chief, hung up, and returned to the table. Bess and George looked baffled when she told them what she'd learned from the chief.

"Roger Cox?" George said. "But he inherited Delia Cox's property. What more could he be hunting for?"

Nancy thought for a minute. "The mansion was sold before Delia died," she recalled. "Legally, it—

and everything in it—belongs to Carl Haddon, not to Roger Cox. Maybe there's something in the house that Roger wants to get his hands on."

"Do you suppose Delia Cox knew he wanted something in the house?" Bess wondered. "Could that be why she sold the house so soon before she died—to keep something out of Roger's hands?"

"Mr. Tyrell said they didn't hit it off too well," Nancy mused.

"Mr. Tyrell also said that Roger was out of town when he called this morning," George said wryly. "Little did he know he was right here in River Heights."

"And he's been here for several days," Bess added. "We saw his car Thursday night. But who knows how long he was here before then?"

Nancy considered. "Jack Ryman said a lot of people were interested in where the Sassoon items had gone. I'll bet Roger Cox was one of them."

"But what's his connection with Margo Rosnick?" George frowned. "Margo told me she'd worked at the bank for five years. I wonder how long she's known Roger Cox."

"Maybe she's the one who told him about his aunt's safe-deposit box," Nancy said.

"But how is Vanessa Chilton tied in?" Bess asked. "Did she buy the Bible to help him?"

Nancy shook her head. "If Cox and Chilton are allies, why would he break into Haddon Hall? Actually, we don't know for sure that Roger Cox was the intruder. But you guys saw his car racing away from the property Thursday night just after I chased the intruder through the woods."

"When was the first break-in? Wednesday night?" George asked.

Nancy nodded. "So my guess is he's been here awhile." She took a last bite of her omelet and pushed her plate away. "We may be able to find out where he's staying. He isn't a River Heights resident, and he probably has no family here, so he should be staying in a hotel."

Bess perked up. "We can get on the phone and call all the motels and hotels in the phone book."

"Let's go to my house. We have two phone lines," George said. "That way we can make the calls twice as fast."

Nancy and her friends quickly paid their bill, left the restaurant, and drove to the Faynes' house. They divided up the list of hotels in the River Heights Yellow Pages. George and Bess used one phone line, while Nancy took the other one alone.

Half an hour later Bess trudged into the bedroom where Nancy was phoning and flopped down on the bed. Nancy ended her call and hung up. The girls traded looks. "George is finishing one more call," Bess reported. "But we asked to be connected to Roger Cox's room at twelve different places so far. Every one said they had no one registered under that name."

"Same story here," Nancy said. "Except at the Atrium Hotel. The operator connected me to a room, but there was no answer. When I asked to leave a message, she realized she'd made a mistake. She thought I'd said Robert Cox."

"That's close," Bess said. "Maybe we should check it out."

"I agree," Nancy said.

George walked into the room, her face shining. "This could be something," she said, waving a piece of paper. "The last place I called, the Lakeside Motel, says they have a Roger Wilcox registered."

Nancy's eyes widened. "Lakeside Motel? I think I know that place. It's just off Windridge—not too far from Haddon Hall. If Roger was planning to break into the school, that would be a logical place to stay. We should check out both places."

"But neither guest is named Roger Cox," George said.

"I wouldn't be surprised if he was traveling under an assumed name, with a fake ID," Nancy said. "The more I see, the more I think we're dealing with an experienced criminal."

"Poor Delia Cox—she had only one relative and he turned out to be a lowlife," Bess said with a sigh.

Nancy nodded. "George, you go to the Atrium and see what you can learn. I'll take the Lakeside Motel. Of the two, I think the Lakeside is the better bet. It's cheaper, for one thing—more affordable for a long stay."

Bess made a face. "But the Lakeside is a dump. No one in his right mind would stay there."

Nancy smiled ruefully. "Maybe Roger Cox is not in his right mind."

Bess swung her car into the parking lot of the Lakeside Motel. Two one-story buildings stretched from either side of a central office, all of them badly in need of fresh paint. A row of blank wooden doors opened onto the littered, potholed parking lot. Between each pair of doors was a square window with grubby flowered curtains. One window had been replaced by a sheet of plywood.

"You're sure you'll be okay here alone?" Bess asked Nancy uneasily.

Nancy patted Bess's hand. "I can take care of myself. Besides, I need you to go talk to Jack Ryman. He must have met Roger Cox at some point. Whatever he can tell us about him could be useful."

After Bess drove away, Nancy strolled into the motel office. Behind a battered Formica counter sat a middle-aged woman in a shapeless blue housedress. She was staring at a small TV and holding a stained coffee mug. "Looking for a room?" she asked, bored eyes flicking up at Nancy.

Nancy put on a cheery smile. "I'm looking for a friend. His name is Roger Wilcox." She hoped the security at this place was as lax as everything else appeared to be.

The desk clerk paused. "Is he expecting you?"

"No. I called, but he wasn't in."

The woman's eyes narrowed. "I'm the operator, too. He doesn't get many calls. When did you phone?"

Nancy faked a ditzy giggle. "I can't remember exactly—yesterday afternoon or evening, I guess. You see, I'm an old friend of his from Nevada."

The woman nodded slowly. "You're not his girl-friend, are you? I don't want any trouble."

Nancy took a chance. "No, but I did fix him up with a friend of mine, a girl with curly brown hair. Margo's her name."

The desk clerk relaxed, as if reassured that Nancy was honestly one of her guest's friends. "Yeah, I've seen her. They hit it off, I guess. She was here most of the weekend." She peered through the blinds. "I don't see his car now, though. He must be out somewhere. You want to leave a message?"

Nancy shook her head. "I'll come back. Thanks anyway." She waved and backed out of the office.

Through the blinds, Nancy had noticed a woman

in jeans and a smock hauling a bag of trash out of one of the guest rooms. Housekeeping staff—that's the best way to learn about a hotel guest, Nancy told herself. She strolled over to the maid.

"Which room is Mr. Cox's—I mean, Mr. Wilcox's?" Nancy asked.

"Twenty-four," the maid said, barely raising her head. She jutted her chin toward a door at the end of the building.

"Have you cleaned it already?"

"It comes next," the woman said. She gave a humorless chuckle as she shut the door of the room she was cleaning. "We only have three rooms booked. I don't mind—saves me work."

Nancy grinned. "Business is slow, huh?" She followed the maid as the woman trundled her rolling cart down the cracked cement walkway.

The woman rolled her eyes. "Look at this place. Would you stay here if you could afford anything better?"

She slid her master key into the lock on the door to room 24. Nancy hung back, but she peered over the woman's shoulder. The room inside looked messy.

The maid emerged with an overflowing wastebasket in her hand. "Mr. Wilcox isn't in," she said to Nancy curiously. "You better come back some other time."

As she tipped the basket into her trash bag, a

crumpled sheet of paper drifted out. Nancy bent to pick it up. Her quick gaze studied it.

The paper was covered with the same scrawled signature, repeated over and over: Delia Cox. Delia Cox. Delia Cox . . .

Why had Roger been practicing his dead aunt's signature?

13

Trapped!

Nancy could scarcely tear her eyes away from the telltale sheet of paper, but she willed herself to act casual. She had to get into Roger Cox's room to search it.

"As I said, I'm a friend of Roger's," Nancy told the maid. She flashed a disarming smile. "I was hoping to leave a present in his room. Sort of a welcome gift. Is that okay?"

The maid's eyes slid toward the run-down motel office. She hates this job, Nancy thought to herself, but she can't afford to lose it. "I can't let just anybody in," the maid said. "How do I know who you are?"

"I'll pop in and out," Nancy promised. "You can watch me the whole time."

The maid let out an exhausted sigh, then gave in. "I guess it's all right. You look like a nice, normal kid." She flipped the light on and allowed Nancy to enter the room ahead of her. "But let me warn you, honey—you shouldn't hang out with a sleazy guy like this Wilcox."

Nancy's ears pricked up. "What's so sleazy about him?"

The maid clucked with disgust. "He stays out all night and sleeps until noon. Some days I can't even get in to clean the room. And he keeps this place a pigsty." She gestured toward the cluttered room. The narrow, lumpy bed was unmade, and clothes had been flung carelessly on a stained armchair. Newspapers were stacked on the dresser, along with empty soda cans and fast-food cartons.

Nancy zipped open her backpack and pulled out a paper bag. Inside it was a half-eaten muffin from that morning. It could pass as a present. She set it atop the TV set on the dresser. "I guess he'll see it there," she said to the maid.

The maid disappeared into the bathroom with her scrubbing brush and disinfectant. Nancy drifted over to the door. She fished out of her pocket the paper napkin on which she'd written Roger Cox's license plate number. She deftly folded it over and over into a thick little package.

Hearing the maid flush the toilet, Nancy hurriedly stuffed the wad of paper into the frame of the door lock. With the tongue of the lock blocked, the mechanism wouldn't click into place when the door was pulled shut.

The maid trudged out of the bathroom. She cast a despairing look around her. "Where to begin?" she muttered. Then she glanced sharply at Nancy. "Done leaving your present?"

Nancy nodded. "Thanks so much." She left the room, blinking as she emerged into the noontime sunlight. Noticing a gas station on the other side of a ragged hedge, Nancy crossed over to it. She bought a cold drink from the soda machine, then sat on a side curb to wait. She kept her eyes trained on Roger Cox's motel room door.

Twenty minutes later the maid shuffled out of room 24. Nancy sprang to her feet to watch. When the woman pulled the door shut behind her, she turned and frowned. "You're right, it didn't click shut," Nancy murmured under her breath. "But please don't check the lock. That slob Roger Cox has made enough extra work for you today. Don't waste any more time on his room."

Almost as if she'd heard Nancy, the maid turned away from the door, shaking her head in exasperation. She took her cleaning cart and rumbled away from room 24.

Nancy crept up to the hedge and peeked through a gap. She watched until the maid disappeared into a supply closet at the other end of the

116

motel. Then Nancy slipped through the hedge, darted across the parking lot, and tried the doorknob of room 24. The door stuck for a moment, then popped open. Nancy ducked through, yanking the wadded paper out of the lock. She quickly shut the door behind her and drew a deep breath of relief.

Though Nancy didn't dare turn on the lights, she could see that the maid had worked wonders inside room 24. The sagging bed was now smoothly made up; newspapers were neatly stacked on the desk, and all the wrappers, bottles, and food-encrusted cartons had been thrown away. Roger Cox's dirty clothes lay folded and piled on the dresser. The grubby flowered carpet had been vacuumed, and the furniture was polished. He owes her a good tip when he checks out, Nancy thought to herself. But I'll bet he won't give her a dime.

Nancy began by checking out the closet, a tiny dark space behind a plain metal door. Wire hangers hung empty on the pole—evidently Roger Cox couldn't bother to hang up his clothes, no matter how long he was staying. A battered vinyl suitcase lay on the floor. Nancy checked inside, but it was empty. The luggage tags were blank; Roger Cox hadn't written in his name or address. She inspected a crumpled baggage check tied to the handle. "Las Vegas, Nevada," Nancy read. "That makes sense."

117

Nancy backed out of the closet and headed for the small table near the door. She sifted through a pile of sports magazines, racing sheets, old lottery tickets, and betting slips from a racetrack near Chicago. "This guy must really believe he has a chance to strike it rich," Nancy murmured. "He only wants to make money the easy way."

Then, at the bottom of the pile, Nancy pulled out a dog-eared photocopy, ringed with coffee stains. "He's sure read this a lot," Nancy murmured. She tilted it toward the window to read it.

At the top of the page was the logo of Midstate Federal Bank. Beneath that was the heading "Safe-Deposit Vault." The rest of the page was ruled into columns. It's a ledger, Nancy guessed.

The first column showed dates. In the second column, various people had printed their names. The third column showed corresponding signatures. The narrow fourth column recorded five-digit numbers, not in any noticeable order.

When Nancy gazed at the dates in the first column her pulse pounded with excitement. These dates recorded safe-deposit vault visits from last November! Margo Rosnick had told George that Delia Cox visited the vault on November fifteenth. "Margo must have given this photocopy to Roger Cox," Nancy said to herself. "That proves she's his accomplice. And they're definitely trying to get into that safe-deposit box."

Nancy looked down the column until she found the date: November 15. Then she traced the row across with her finger. There it was, the name Delia Cox printed in a shaky hand. In the next column, in loopy, old-fashioned handwriting, was the elderly woman's signature.

It perfectly matched the copies Nancy had seen on the paper in Roger Cox's wastebasket.

Nancy glanced at the fourth column and realized that those five-digit numbers must be the account numbers. She read the number after Delia Cox's signature: 49987. She reached inside her T-shirt and fished out the chain with the brass key. She flipped it over. For the first time she noticed five tiny faint numbers imprinted on the key—49987. She could barely make them out, but they were there. It was a match!

Suddenly she heard a jiggling metallic sound at the door. She crouched, peering over her shoulder. Roger Cox had returned!

The door flew open, and a man with shaggy dark hair burst into the room. His eyes lit up when he saw Nancy. "Well, what have we here?" he snickered. "Miss Nancy Drew, I presume. And what was that in your hand?"

Nancy dropped the key back inside her shirt. "Oh, nothing!" she said blithely.

"Don't lie to me," Cox snarled. He gave the door a vicious kick, slamming it shut behind him. "I was

119

wondering how to get that key from you—and here you've brought it right to me. This sure is my lucky day!"

"I don't know what you're talking about—" Nancy began.

Roger Cox lumbered toward her, a cruel sneer on his blunt-featured face. "Jack Ryman told me a girl found a safe-deposit key in Sarah Sassoon's old jacket," he said. "That was before Ryman got suspicious and clammed up. I got your phone number and address from that woman at the secondhand clothes store."

"Was that *you* at my house Saturday night?"

Cox gave a taunting chuckle. "Well, I had to try to break in. But give me credit—I first tried to buy the jacket and key from you fair and square. Or at least Margo tried."

"Margo Rosnick," Nancy said. "She was working with you all along."

"At least from Friday on," he said. "But once I had her charmed, she was very helpful. Except you didn't show up to meet her." Ryman took a step toward Nancy. "And then your foolish housekeeper kept me from taking the key from your house. So now I have to get it from you the hard way."

Roger Cox suddenly flung himself at Nancy. Though she sidestepped quickly, he still caught her by the shoulders. His heavyset body threw her off balance. They grappled for a moment; then he tackled Nancy and flung her to the floor.

"I won't give you the key!" Nancy said through clenched teeth.

"You won't have a choice," Cox grunted. He twisted her arm behind her. Nancy bit back a cry of pain.

The burly man rose and heaved Nancy onto his hip and lugged her toward the closet. Nancy struggled, flailing at him with her other fist. Cox trapped her free arm under his elbow. He wrestled her into the closet, flinging her against the back wall and slamming the metal door shut.

Nancy crouched in the tiny dark space, wondering what Cox planned to do. Why hadn't he ripped the key off her chain and taken off with it?

Only a thin line of light seeped in through the crack below the door. She could hear Cox's labored breathing on the other side of the door. Then came scrapes and thumps as a piece of furniture was banged against the door. Nancy guessed that he had wedged a chair under the knob to trap her inside. She sank down unhappily on the vinyl suitcase.

"Don't do this, Roger," she called through the door. "You'll end up in jail. Why risk that? You can get into that safe-deposit box legally. After all, you're Delia Cox's legal heir."

Roger Cox replied with a snort of contempt.

"You mean I should call Evan Tyrell? I know the drill—he'd need a request in writing, then he'd have to verify the box's ownership with the bank, and then amend the estate's original accounting. Well, I can't wait that long."

"Why not?" Nancy waited, but she got no reply. "Roger?" She pressed her ear to the door. She thought she heard footsteps on the tile floor of the bathroom. A few seconds later she heard a gurgle, as if liquid were being poured. What was he doing?

Then the strip of light at the bottom of the door disappeared. Nancy saw the edge of a white towel stuffed into the crack. A familiar, sickeningly sweet odor rose from the towel.

Chloroform! He was trying to knock her out.

Nancy looked quickly around her dark cell, estimating how long it would take for the fumes to build up in that tiny space. She stood up, to be as far from the fumes as possible.

Roger Cox's voice broke into her thoughts. "I can't afford to let you snoop around anymore," he declared. "What if something happened—like you found another will, leaving my aunt's money to somebody else?"

Nancy stiffened. "Is that likely?"

"I don't know," he answered with a growl. "I saw Aunt Delia stuff a paper into a drawer the day the movers cleared out the mansion. That's what I was hunting for when I broke into the school."

So Roger *was* the intruder, Nancy thought.

"It'd be just like that old crone to cut me out," Roger went on, "just because I wanted to build houses on the estate."

Nancy felt light-headed. Cox's words swirled around her as he continued, "I saw you trying to talk your way into Haddon Hall on Sunday, and I figured you were on the trail of the second will. I knew that Jack Ryman had helped you—that's why I threw the brick at your car that afternoon, to keep you from getting any more leads from him."

"I don't know anything about a second will," Nancy said. She fought to keep her head clear.

"I can't risk having anyone find it," Roger complained. He sounded angry and bitter. "I owe a lot of money to some pretty rough characters, and they're not known for their patience. . . ."

That was the last thing Nancy heard before she blacked out.

14

A Narrow Escape

Slowly Nancy became conscious that she was in a moving car. How can that be? I'm lying down, she thought groggily. She opened her eyes, but all she could see was the underside of a cheap brown acrylic blanket. She recognized it—from the bed in Roger Cox's motel room.

So he's kidnapped me, Nancy thought grimly. Adding one more serious crime to the counts against him.

Struggling to shift positions, Nancy realized that her hands and feet were bound with strips of cotton. Roger must have ripped up the linens in his motel room, she guessed. Another strip had been tied across her mouth as a gag.

Nancy lay still, resting her cheek against the

scratchy plush of the car seat. She wriggled her shoulders, testing to see whether the silver chain that held the safe-deposit key was still there. It wasn't. She did feel pricks of pain from several tiny lacerations around her throat. Roger must have ripped the chain right off her, frantic to get his hands on the key.

Well, at least he didn't leave me trapped in that airless closet, Nancy reasoned. But where is he taking me—and why? She willed herself to concentrate on the car's motion, hoping to learn where she was going.

Sunlight fell on the brown blanket in flashes. That means we're moving through a wooded area, Nancy reckoned. The car swerved around a left-hand curve. Then she felt it swing up a short, steep rise and swoop downward again. Ticklebelly Bridge! Nancy thought. As she expected, the car swung next around a sharp right curve. Now she knew where she was. Cox was taking her out Windridge Road, past Haddon Hall.

A moment later she was tossed abruptly into the air as the car struck a pothole. I know that pothole—it's just past the school's front gates, Nancy remembered. *So he's not going into the school.* Where, then?

The car then took an unexpected lurch to the left. Nancy was thrown from the seat onto the floor. She arched her back uncomfortably over the hump in the middle. Despite herself, she let out a grunt as the car bounced over rough terrain. She could hear sticks and branches whip against the sides of the car. It was a good guess that Roger was driving off the road and into some woods.

Nancy fought to keep her mental map clear. Haddon Hall's property goes on for another quarter mile past the gates, she remembered. So when we turned left, we drove onto school land. Roger must have found another entrance and managed to leave it open.

Finally the car jerked to a stop. Nancy heard the engine switch off and the driver's-side door open. She felt Roger Cox's weight shift off the front seat as he climbed out. Then, abruptly, he yanked open the door near Nancy's feet. He took hold of her bound ankles and hauled her from the car. Nancy writhed in his grasp, twisting her body to keep her head from striking the steel doorframe. "Oh, so you're awake now, huh?" he growled. "Guess I should have used more chloroform."

Nancy cringed as she was dragged over the rough ground. A short distance from the car, Roger dropped her ankles. He pulled off the blanket with a taunting flourish. "I couldn't leave you at the motel—your nosy friends would have known where to find you," he sneered. "So welcome to my home away from home. I got to know these woods pretty well—they made a convenient place to hide while I was, ah, visiting Haddon Hall. I'll really miss this place." He gave a short, harsh laugh.

Nancy made a few muffled grunts. Roger crossed his arms and smirked at her. "Sorry, I couldn't understand you. What next, you're asking? Well, now that I have the key and I can forge my dear auntie's signature, I'll get into her safe-deposit box at last. Everything will look official, so dumb little Margo won't lose her job in the end. You see, she thinks we're going to use the money to get married and start a home. What a loser! By the time Margo realizes I've been using her, I'll be way out of town."

Nancy glared coldly at Roger. His lip curled in contempt and he gave her a shove with his foot. "The way Aunt Delia talked about it," he bragged, "I figure that box is full of gold bars or jewels or something priceless. I'll cash it in back in Vegas, pay off my debts, and still have a fortune to spare. The money I inherited from the sale of the house just didn't go far enough."

He turned to stride back to his car. "Don't worry, babe," he called over his shoulder to Nancy. "Someone will find you soon enough. Of course, this estate covers one hundred acres, and most of the time no one even comes into this part. By the time they find you, you might be dead, but I won't be around to attend your funeral. So long, sweetie. I have to get to the bank before it closes."

Roger jumped into his car and slammed the door. He started the engine with a defiant roar. Lurching forward, he swung around Nancy, then crashed back through the trees, the same way he'd come.

Nancy rolled onto her back. After sliding her arms under her body and pulling her legs through, Nancy had her hands in front of her. She checked her watch. It was almost two o'clock. Bess and George would be wondering why she hadn't called them to pick her up. Maybe they had already cruised past the Lakeside Motel, looking for her. But how long would it take them or anyone to think of searching the woods around the school?

Frustrated, Nancy flung her head back against the ground. She couldn't wait that long. Roger would get to Midstate Federal Bank before three o'clock, its closing time. After that, Nancy guessed, he would head out of town as fast as he could— maybe he'd even leave the country. She had to reach the bank before he disappeared with the loot from the safe-deposit box!

She glanced down at the cotton strips lashed around her wrists. Then, under her wrists, she noticed her belt buckle—the silver dragon-shaped buckle she'd bought from the Telltale Heart. The edges of the dragon were thin, hard, and sharp. But would they cut through a sheet?

Nancy vigorously began to saw away at her bonds. The buckle sliced through the cloth. Thank goodness Lakeside uses cheap linens and keeps using them until they're ready to fall apart! Nancy thought with delight.

Her hands were free in a minute, and her feet soon after. She reached back to untie the gag from her mouth, then rubbed her feet, urging the blood back into them. Then she jumped up and pivoted, trying to guess in which direction to run. She had no time to lose floundering around in the forest.

"Windridge Road runs along the east edge of the property," Nancy murmured. "And we drove past the gates before we turned. So I must be northeast of the main buildings. That means I have to go southwest to reach them."

She stepped over to a nearby oak. "There's no moss here to show me which side of the tree is north," she mused, "but the bark is thicker on this side, which is always the north side. So I'll head the opposite way." Moving tentatively, she gazed up through the trees to check the position of the sun. In springtime, she knew, the sun was never directly overhead, but in the southern half of the sky. Still, by two o'clock it should be moving into the west. To head southwest, then, she should go toward the sun.

Moving faster, she sensed that the ground was sloping uphill. That makes sense—those sketches I saw of the housing development showed that the main mansion was on the crest of a hill, she recalled. She began to jog ahead confidently.

About five minutes later she heard voices—kids' voices, calling out to one another. She broke out of the woods onto a long green slope of lawn. Ahead of her was a squad of students in gym clothes, practicing with lacrosse sticks. They halted and stared at her. Their phys ed teacher blew her whistle in surprise.

Nancy trotted toward the mansion, trying to ignore their stares. From the corner of her eye she saw Vernon, the groundskeeper, coiling up a long green hose at the edge of the playing field. He straightened up, caught sight of Nancy, and marched angrily toward her.

Nancy speeded up, but Vernon moved fast enough to seize her arm before she reached the front door. "Ms. Chilton's going to deal with you," he said. "I recognize you—you're that reporter who's been trying to get in here for days."

"Fine, take me to Ms. Chilton," Nancy said. "But hurry!"

As they hustled through the front door, Vanessa Chilton was already striding into the entry hall. She must have seen Nancy from her window. Her sharp, lined face was set in a scowl. "You again!" she exclaimed.

"Call the police," Nancy pleaded.

"I certainly will," the headmistress said coldly.

"It's about time," Vernon added.

The headmistress stalked down the hallway to

the library. Nancy hurried after her. "Ask for Chief McGinnis," Nancy said, "and tell him Nancy Drew is with you. He knows me."

"I gather you've been arrested before," Ms. Chilton said tartly.

"No, I'm a detective," Nancy said. "And I know who's been breaking into your school. The same man just kidnapped me and left me tied up in your woods. And he stole something from me—something important."

In the library doorway Ms. Chilton halted. She swung around to face Nancy, light dawning in her eyes. "So that's why you were snooping." She paused, then dashed over to the phone on the library desk and handed the receiver to Nancy.

Nancy quickly dialed Chief McGinnis. He agreed to dispatch officers to Midstate Federal Bank to catch Roger. "We should be in time to nab him coming out of the bank. Let's hope he has the contents of the box in his possession," he said. "Meet us there as soon as you can, Nancy."

"Will do," Nancy promised. As soon as she'd hung up, though, she realized that she didn't have a car. "I've got to meet the police downtown at Midstate Federal Bank," she said, turning to Ms. Chilton. "Can I call a taxi to take me there?"

"Taxi? No way!" the headmistress declared. "I'll drive you myself. My car is right out front. Vernon, run to my office and fetch my purse."

"Yes, ma'am," the groundskeeper said. He hurried out of the library.

"Oh, you don't need to—" Nancy began.

"Nonsense," Ms. Chilton said. "I have as much at stake in catching this thief as you do. But why Midstate Federal?"

"I'll explain on the way," Nancy said. "But basically, he's trying to open a safe-deposit box, using a brass key he took from me. It was one of the things he was looking for when he broke in here."

Ms. Chilton's eyes widened. "A key?" she said. "A brass key—like this one?"

She stepped over to the huge oil portrait of the glamorous young woman. Reaching underneath the ornate gilded frame, she pulled out an identical brass key. Nancy's jaw dropped.

"I found this taped here when we first moved in," Ms. Chilton explained. "I was admiring the portrait. She was the former owner of this mansion." Her eyes softened as she stared at the painting. "Wasn't she beautiful?"

Just then a chill ran up Nancy's spine. Her eyes flickered from the headmistress's face to the portrait and back. So that was why the portrait had looked familiar to her!

Ms. Chilton looked so much like Sarah Sassoon. Could she be the mysterious long-lost Sassoon relative?

15

Betrayed by Love

Vanessa Chilton saw the astonished look on Nancy's face and guessed her thoughts. A shy smile crept onto her face. "Yes," she said softly. "I am Sarah Sassoon's niece. Grandniece, actually. My grandmother was her sister—Stella Sassoon."

"What was her middle name?" Nancy asked.

Ms. Chilton looked baffled. "Helen. Why?"

"S.H.S.," Nancy murmured. "We found her initials on a blouse."

"Really?" Ms. Chilton said eagerly. "May I see it sometime?"

Just then Vernon returned with the headmistress's purse. "Thanks," she said. "Now we'd better hurry, Miss Drew. You can tell me the rest of your story in the car."

"Only if *you* tell *me* the rest of the Sassoon family history," Nancy replied.

Once in the car, Nancy was impressed by Vanessa Chilton's driving skill. The headmistress expertly handled the curves of Windridge Road as they sped toward town. "If a police officer stops us, will Chief McGinnis vouch that we were driving fast on his orders?" she asked Nancy with a wry smile.

"I think so," Nancy said. "Now, about your grandmother . . ."

"Right." Ms. Chilton gripped the steering wheel firmly. "Well, the villain of the story is Sarah and Stella's father, Jacob Sassoon. I guess he was a real tyrant. He'd inherited a small fortune and made it into a big one. Everyone in the family had to live the way he wanted them to. His two daughters were sent east, away from River Heights, to boarding school. He wanted them to mix only with the children of the 'best' families—by which he meant rich families."

"And did they?"

Ms. Chilton shook her head. "Sarah never married, as you know. Her father convinced her that no one was good enough for her. But Stella, my grandmother, had a mind of her own. In college, she fell in love with a Milwaukee man named John Chilton. He was on scholarship—his mother was a poor widow. And he planned a career as a teacher, not a business tycoon."

134

"That must have driven Jacob crazy," Nancy guessed.

"It sure did—especially since Stella was secretly his favorite."

"Poor Sarah!"

Ms. Chilton nodded. "Stella and her dad had a dreadful fight. He forbade her from marrying John Chilton, but she defied him by eloping. She thought her father loved her so much that he'd forgive her, but he cut her off without a penny. And Stella was just as proud and stubborn as her father. She refused to ask his forgiveness. They never spoke again. He never even knew about his grandson, my father, John Chilton Jr., who was born in 1947."

"So he scratched your grandmother's name out of the family Bible," Nancy murmured.

Vanessa Chilton impatiently swerved around a slow-moving car. They were in thicker traffic now, approaching downtown. "How did you know?" she asked.

"My friend Bess saw the Bible at Past Times Books," Nancy explained.

"Why, that's where I found it," the headmistress said, surprised. "You see, I was hunting for family heirlooms. Carl Haddon told me the name of the dealer who took all the Sassoon belongings from the mansion."

"Jack Ryman."

Ms. Chilton threw an admiring glance at Nancy. "Wow, you are good."

Nancy waved away the compliment. "But tell me, how did you wind up at Haddon Hall? By coincidence?"

"Not a bit." Ms. Chilton sped through an intersection, just beating the red light. "I read in a teachers' magazine that Haddon Hall was moving to River Heights and looking for a new headmistress. I knew the Sassoons came from River Heights, so I applied for the job."

Spotting a blocked intersection ahead, she detoured swiftly down a side street. "My family taught us to hate the Sassoons," she went on, "but I was secretly curious about them. After all, they were part of who I am. My grandparents are gone now. Actually my parents are too; they were killed in a plane crash eight years ago. I needed to connect with my heritage. So imagine how thrilled I was when I found that Haddon Hall was in the Sassoons' own house!"

"But Carl Haddon had already cleared out the family belongings," Nancy said.

Vanessa Chilton sighed. "True. But I was still in my grandmother's girlhood home, with a picture of my great-aunt Sarah in the library. And with a little detective work, I knew I could find other heirlooms."

She steered around a corner onto River Avenue.

A block ahead was Midstate Federal. Nancy could see a knot of squad cars parked in front, lights flashing. "The police are here," she said, relieved. "I wonder if they've apprehended Roger yet."

Just as Vanessa Chilton swung over to the curb, Nancy saw the front door of the bank begin to swing open. Two figures appeared in the doorway—then darted back inside. "He saw the squad cars," Nancy guessed. She jumped out of Ms. Chilton's car and ran toward the bank.

A police officer had whipped out her gun and was crouching behind her open car door. She called, "Come on out, Cox!"

He won't come out the front door now, Nancy's instincts told her. Cox always thinks he can beat the odds. She followed a pair of officers peeling off down an alley to the parking lot in back.

As they swung around the back corner of the bank building, Nancy saw Roger Cox charging out the back entrance. In front of him stumbled Margo Rosnick, one arm twisted behind her back. Roger Cox gripped her wrist cruelly. Nancy caught her breath. She saw the gun in his other hand, pressed against the woman's curly brown hair. He had taken Margo hostage!

Terrified, she cried out, "But, Roger, you won't shoot me. You love me!"

Roger Cox laughed in reply.

Using Margo as a shield, Cox started to run

toward his gray car. A police officer lunged forward, blocking his path.

Roger wheeled and glanced wildly around him. He caught sight of a metal fire escape, bolted to the exterior of the bank building. He gave Margo a fierce jerk and dragged her toward the dangling bottom steps. "Dumb move," Nancy muttered under her breath. "You can go up, but you won't get away. Surrender, Roger, before the girl gets hurt!"

Roger Cox shoved his gun into the waist of his pants, then pulled down the hanging section of fire escape and forced Margo onto it. He grabbed his gun again and jabbed it into the small of her back. With a whimper, Margo scurried ahead of him up the metal rungs.

Nancy studied the fire escape. It climbed to the top of the four-story building, then disappeared over a carved stone parapet onto the flat roof.

She heard an officer call through a bullhorn, "Surrender, Cox. Don't make us shoot."

"If you fire, the girl will die!" Cox shouted back as he climbed the escape. There was an edge of hysteria to his voice.

Nancy quickly studied the buildings on either side of Midstate Federal. The one to the left was about the same height and had a small roof structure with a door. She sidled over to the officer with the bullhorn. "Keep him talking—distract him," she muttered. "Give me a chance to get up there with him. I've already dealt with this guy—I may be able to talk him into surrendering."

"At least get him to let the girl go," the officer suggested. "Then we can take him by force."

Nancy raced into the adjacent building. Luck was with her. An elevator car was waiting, empty, on the ground floor. She took it to the top. As she dashed off, she saw a doorway marked To Roof. She ran over, opened it, and hurried up the short flight of stairs.

Bursting out onto the roof, Nancy saw that Roger's back was to her. He was still holding Margo tightly in front of him, the gun against her temple. Her face was drained of color, and her body was stiff. She twisted in his grip and caught sight of Nancy. Nancy signaled her to be quiet.

Creeping to the edge of the adjacent roof, Nancy scooped up a handful of loose gravel. She locked gazes with Margo, warning her silently to be ready to make a move. Then Nancy tossed the gravel onto the Midstate roof.

The hail of tiny pebbles startled Cox. He flinched and jerked toward the sound.

Margo Rosnick bolted from his grasp in a split second. She ran desperately toward Nancy's roof. She coiled her muscles and leaped into the air, across the gap between the two buildings.

She fell short by six inches.

Nancy gasped and reached out, but she missed Margo's flailing hand. Scrambling wildly, Margo tried to grab hold of the building as she plunged downward. She tore her fingers against the rough stone but couldn't find anything to grip.

"Serves you right!" Roger Cox crowed.

Then he swiveled toward Nancy, his eyes narrowing with anger. "How did you get here, you interfering fool? Well, if I can't shoot her, I'll shoot you!" he swore.

He raised his gun and aimed it straight at Nancy.

16

Heir Apparent

Nancy stared down the barrel of Roger Cox's gun. She doubted she could reason with him—not with that crazy glint in his eye. She had to try, though.

"Roger," she began, "why spoil everything? You opened the safe-deposit box, right?"

"Yeah—some fortune." Roger spat angrily to one side. "Aunt Delia told me the Sassoon fortune was hidden from me. Crazy old crone—there was nothing in that box but worthless stocks from some defunct adding machine company. Now I'm really mad, and somebody's gonna pay."

He fired a shot at Nancy. She ducked behind the parapet just before a bullet whizzed over her head.

Then Nancy heard a wild squeal of tires on the

street, followed by the blare of a car horn. Nancy recognized it. Bess!

Roger sprang to the edge of the roof and looked down. From behind the parapet, Nancy glimpsed a dark blue cap with a badge right at the top of the fire escape. Roger hadn't noticed yet that the police were creeping closer.

I've got to distract him, give them time to sneak up on him, Nancy thought. She popped up above the parapet. "Hey, Roger!"

He wheeled around, swinging his pistol in front of him. Nancy ducked, then bobbed up again. Roger fired another reckless shot.

One officer leaped forward, knocking the gun out of Roger's hand. The other tackled him from behind. Pinning him to the roof, the officer snapped the handcuffs onto Cox's wrists. Then the police hauled him to his feet, shoved him into the building, and took him down in the elevator.

Nancy let out her breath, then ran down the building's inside stairs to street level. Roger was being put into a squad car, his head hanging low.

A crowd had gathered in the alley around Margo. She was sitting up, wincing with pain. "My leg—I think it's broken," she moaned to a woman officer.

"You're lucky it was nothing more serious," the officer told her. "A fall from the fourth story. I radioed for an ambulance, and it should be here soon." Seeing Nancy, the officer shook her hand. "Thanks for your help. I'll go with Ms. Rosnick in the ambulance."

"Will you release her from the hospital?" Nancy asked.

The officer shook her head. "She'll be arrested as an accessory."

Seeing Bess and George push through the onlookers, Nancy nodded toward them. "My friends and I should be called as witnesses." She wrote their names and phone numbers on the officer's pad.

Bess tugged urgently on Nancy's elbow. She waved a piece of paper in her other hand. "Nancy, hurry, look what I found!" she exclaimed.

Nancy grinned. "Am I glad to see you! How did you know to come here?"

"When I went back to the Lakeside Motel and you weren't there," Bess said, "I figured something was up. I picked up George at the Atrium and headed here. Just a hunch."

George pulled a twig from Nancy's red-gold hair. "Where were you?"

Nancy grimaced. "Roger abducted me and stashed me in the woods near Haddon Hall. But Ms. Chilton helped me get here. And guess what, guys?"

"No, my news first," Bess said impatiently. "This

143

is *huge,* Nancy. You see, Jack Ryman told me that that rosewood bed and nightstand were from Delia Cox's own bedroom, so I went to the antique store to check them again. I looked in the drawer of the nightstand. At first it seemed empty, but then I noticed it didn't slide in all the way. I slid the drawer out and reached way in the back and found something jamming the drawer." She held up a folded paper. "Somehow it got wedged up inside. Neither the antique store owner nor Jack Ryman had seen it."

Nancy reached for the paper. "What is it?"

"Read it." Bess clenched her hands in excitement as Nancy unfolded it.

Nancy's eyes swept over the typed sheet. "'I, Delia Cox, being of sound mind and body . . .'" she began. She glanced at the bottom of the document. "Bess, this is a will—dated November eighteenth, the day Delia Cox died. Her final will!"

"And, look, it's properly signed and has two witnesses and everything," Bess pointed out. "That must mean it's legal."

"This must be the paper Roger saw his aunt put in the drawer the day the movers were at the mansion." Nancy scanned it quickly. "It says Delia bequeaths everything she inherited from Sarah Sassoon back to the Sassoon family."

"And she authorized her executors to search for Stella Sassoon's heirs," Bess added.

144

"Who's Stella Sassoon?" George wondered.

"That's my news," Nancy said eagerly. "Stella Sassoon was Sarah's sister. And you'll never guess who her granddaughter is."

Just then Vanessa Chilton walked over to Nancy's side. "Miss Drew, what's up?" she asked innocently. "Good news?"

Nancy flashed her an excited smile. "Very good news, I think, Ms. Chilton. Can we talk?"

Carson Drew leaned over to pour Vanessa Chilton a second cup of coffee. The Drews had invited the headmistress to their house for dinner a week and a half after Roger Cox's arrest.

"Well, Ms. Chilton," Nancy's father said, "the judge ruled today that Delia Cox's second will is valid. Neither of the two witnesses was disqualified by any conflict of interest—neither one benefited from the will in any way. And Delia's signature was judged to be authentic."

"It looked just like the one I saw on the safe-deposit vault register," Nancy put in.

Evan Tyrell leaned back from the dining table. "I interviewed both witnesses myself," he said. "They testified that Delia was of sound mind when she signed it."

"Who were they?" George wondered.

"One was Yumiko Sakata, the private nurse

who took care of Delia during her last month," Mr. Tyrell explained. "The other was Alex Magnano."

"Like the Magnano Brothers moving company? I see their vans all over town," Bess said.

Tyrell nodded. "Alex was at the house that morning, supervising his moving crew. Nurse Sakata was helping Delia pack to move to a nursing home."

"She never got there, poor thing." Bess sighed.

"What happened?" Vanessa Chilton's eyes darkened with concern.

"Nurse Sakata remembers Roger Cox arriving," Tyrell explained. "She says he had a furious quarrel with his aunt. Delia finally made him leave, but the quarrel brought on heart palpitations. The nurse rushed her straight to the hospital. She died there that night."

"So much for Roger's story about reconciling with her on her deathbed," Carson Drew added wryly.

"I'll bet Delia meant to take the will out of the drawer once Roger left," Nancy mused, smoothing out a wrinkle in the tablecloth. "Then she could have delivered it to your office, Mr. Tyrell."

"Instead it was left in the drawer, and the moving men took the nightstand away," Hannah said. She passed a plate of cookies to Mr. Tyrell. "If not for Bess, the will might have stayed in that drawer forever."

146

"What a coincidence. If Nancy hadn't found that key in her pocket . . ." George began.

Nancy smiled and shrugged her shoulders inside the satin jacket. She'd worn it in honor of the occasion.

"Oh, that's another thing Nurse Sakata told me," Mr. Tyrell recalled. He took a cookie from the plate and passed it on. "She saw Delia sewing the pocket of an old jacket of Sarah's one day last fall—right after Delia heard about Roger's scheme for developing the Sassoon property. Delia's fingers were bent with arthritis by then, and she could barely see."

Hannah chuckled. "That explains the clumsy stitches."

"Nurse Sakata asked what she was up to, but the old lady wouldn't say," Tyrell said. "Then she wondered why Delia insisted on taking that jacket with her to the nursing home. Now we know—Delia was determined to carry with her a clue to the Sassoon wealth."

"But her suitcase must have been left behind when she was rushed to the hospital," Nancy guessed. "So it got thrown in with the other stuff going to Jack Ryman."

"Well, I'm glad her clue was found in the end," Vanessa Chilton declared. "It got you girls searching, and the will was finally found. Now I'm officially the Sassoon heir. I feel that the rift in the family has been healed at last."

"But that beautiful old house was sold. It could have been yours!" Bess protested.

Ms. Chilton shrugged. "It's better off being a school. I don't care about the Sassoon money. I'm content, even if Roger gambled away the money from the sale of the house and all I've inherited is a few worthless stocks in a safe-deposit box."

Evan Tyrell crooked an eyebrow. "Worthless?"

Nancy nodded. "Roger Cox told me the box held nothing but a few stock certificates from a defunct adding machine company."

Mr. Tyrell smiled. "Right—Portman Adding Machines. Maybe you know it better by its current name—Poradco."

George gasped. "You mean the big computer makers?"

Mr. Tyrell nodded. "I've made some calls to check what those shares are worth. First of all, there have been a few stock splits since then. Each share the Sassoons owned now represents hundreds of shares. What's more, one share of Portman Adding Machines was worth eighty-five cents in 1955. But a share of Poradco is now worth forty-two dollars."

Nancy turned excitedly to Vanessa Chilton. The headmistress's mouth hung open in shock. "Oh, my goodness!" Ms. Chilton exclaimed. "I used to be a math teacher, but I can't add that up at the moment."

Carson Drew laughed. "No need to add it up right now. It's enough to know that you will be a wealthy woman once the final accounting is made."

"Delia Cox knew what she was doing, after all," Hannah Gruen declared, folding her napkin. She reached over and patted Nancy's blue satin sleeve. "She left a clue where Nancy Drew could find it. And the rest is history."